THE MAN
WITHOUT A GUN

**Center Point
Large Print**

Also by Lauran Paine and available from Center Point Large Print:

Corral Canyon
Gundown
Long Bow
Longhorn Trail
The Guns of Parral
The Gunsmith

THE MAN WITHOUT A GUN

A Western Duo

Lauran Paine

CENTER POINT PUBLISHING
THORNDIKE, MAINE

A Circle Ⓥ Western published by
Center Point Large Print in co-operation with
Golden West Literary Agency.

The text of this Large Print edition is unabridged.
In other aspects, this book may vary
from the original edition.
Printed in the United States of America
on permanent paper.
Set in 16-point Times New Roman type.

ISBN: 978-1-60285-932-6

Library of Congress Cataloging-in-Publication Data

Paine, Lauran.
The man without a gun : a Western duo / Lauran Paine. — 1st ed.
    p. cm.
ISBN 978-1-60285-932-6 (lib. bdg. : alk. paper)
1. Large type books. I. Paine, Lauran. Crescent scar. II. Title.
PS3566.A34M275 2010
813′.54—dc22

                                                    2010031221

TABLE OF CONTENTS

The Crescent Scar

I

Barbed wire was just beginning to show up on the range. In fact, the first that most of the riders ever saw of it was on each side of the railroad tracks where it came down out of the Tecate Mountains, ran along the smooth, gently undulating Estacado plains, and disappeared away off in the distance where they began the laborious climb over the Mogollons.

That wire was new, and, when the sun shone on it, it sparkled like a thin spider web of silver, four strands high, that rose and fell endlessly as it followed the contours of the great grassy land, coming out of nowhere and going into the vast beyond. There had been the usual amount of squawking from the cow outfits. In the first place, the railroad track was bad enough to cross, but with the wire up there was no way to get the cattle into the oak-studded little hillocks on the far side of the track. The officials of the railroad company had, at first, just shrugged. They claimed that the cattle were always on the tracks, where they either slowed up the schedules or treed the train crews who tried to run them off afoot, and, since the railroad owned all the sections bordering their track, and the cattle actually were trespassing on railroad land anyway, the cattlemen didn't have a legal leg to stand on.

What the railroad said was true enough, except for one thing—the Estacado country was open range land, which meant if a land owner didn't want someone else's cattle on his land, he had to fence them out—the cowmen didn't have to fence them in. And the upshot of the affair was that the cowmen defeated the purpose of the railroad fence by cutting convenient holes in the fences where they'd drive their cattle across the tracks to the other side, when the feed got short. Even this wouldn't have caused much trouble except that the damned, contrary critters would usually wander back through the fence and bed down on the tracks, lounging and chewing their cuds, oblivious to the huffing, belching iron monsters that howled and steamed and grumbled at them. The leery, profane crew men, who would throw rocks and curse and wave their arms, but who wouldn't get too close because those cattle would take after a man afoot quicker than they'd chase a dog, were thoroughly disliked.

It was a peculiar state of affairs but, except for the irate name-calling and inconvenience to both factions, it wasn't a dangerous situation at all. At least, it wasn't until Sadler Carrel bought out the huge old Garcia holdings, overhauled the run-down ranch, and imported pure-bred Hereford bulls, shorn ones at that, and set up in the cow business.

Then things began to happen. The first danger

point was when a train was sweating out a bunch of Carrel cows, half Mexican and ornery as they come, with a handsome big, slow, easy-going Hereford bull with them. As usual, the train crew was hurling rocks and cursing, and in general annoying the cattle enough to make them get off the tracks, when four Carrel cowboys rode up. Without a word one of the riders shot his .45 and the bullet kicked up dust in front of the train crew. That started it.

When the train pulled into Isabelita, the crew quit to a man. Putting up with the cattle was nerve-wracking enough, but for what they got paid they weren't going to get shot at, too. The railroad company sent two high-powered executives out to call on Sadler Carrel. They found him basking in the late morning sun in front of his new pole corrals with two of his lean-hipped, wide-shouldered riders, discussing a little band of cattle inside the pens.

Sadler Carrel wasn't very tall, possibly not over five feet nine inches, but he had the massive upper arms and the slightly sloping shoulders of a powerful man. His face was pleasant without being distinguished and he was polite to the executives. He even asked them to come up to the house where his Chinese cook would make them a pot of coffee. He smiled easily and told them that was the best he could offer because he was a bachelor.

11

"Mister Carrel, some of your men fired on one of our train crews."

Sadler looked quizzically at the red-faced executive and his eyes were wide and guileless. "Well, I sort of figured we could discuss this in a more leisurely manner. You know . . . like gentlemen." His voice was quietly good-natured.

"When that crew got to Isabelita, they all quit." The railroad company men were showing just the right amount of indignation. Not filled with wrath or appeasing, just a little of both. Carrel appreciated their attitude as he thumbed his black Stetson to the back of his head and hunkered down with his back against a warm green pole of the corral.

"I'm sorry, gentlemen, that you lost your crew, but on the other hand I don't want my cattle stoned and chased."

One of the visitors grunted wryly. "From what I hear, the chasing is the other way around." The man hadn't spoken before. He was Edward Borein, a member of the board of directors and a very wealthy as well as influential man on the line. He lived in Isabelita, a widower, with a half-grown son and a fully grown daughter. "Carrel, this foolishness has got to stop. Our fences are constantly being cut, our schedules are delayed so that shippers lose money, which, in turn costs us money, and we've come to you for assurance that there will be no repetitions of this latest outrage." He wagged his head. "Remember, Carrel, those men of yours were trespassing on railroad company property when they rode up."

Sadler Carrel looked away from Borein. He began methodically to roll a cigarette and the silence was awkward to the railroad men. It was a full minute before he answered, then his cigarette was sending up a thin, blue spiral of smoke above his narrowed, expressionless eyes, as he thoughtfully looked over the visitors. His eyes finally settled on the bulkier of the two men. He recognized him as the leader and spokesman.

"What's your name?"

"Edward Borein. I'm. . . ."

Carrel shook his head peremptorily and interrupted. "I don't care who you are, Mister Borein. All I am interested in is who I've got to do business with." Again there was a pause and the trickle of smoke spiraled lazily upward. "Listen, Mister Borein, there's been trouble ever since you put up that damned fence."

Borein protested: "But no shooting."

Carrel nodded his head slightly. "But no shooting," he repeated. "Not up to now, anyway." He shifted a little on his boot heels and the musical tinkle of his silver-inlaid spurs rang softly with his movement. "The other ranchers hereabouts have been content to cuss at you from a distance and cut your fences. That's not my way of doing business. I won't cut your fences, Mister Borein, but if you don't build crossings for my cattle and quit chousing them with rocks, I'll tear down a mile of your damned fence, posts and all, and pile it on your tracks!"

When Carrel finished speaking, there was a long, tense silence. Borein and his companion were looking steadily into the placid blue eyes of Sadler Carrel and the indifferent, casual slant of the rancher's jaw jutted just a tiny bit toward them. Borein was angry. Carrel was a newcomer in the country and he was making fight talk right from the start. He frowned and held himself in tightly.

"Mister Carrel, if you touch that fence, or trespass on the sections of railroad land that border the tracks, or run your cattle over there, I'll swear out a warrant for your arrest."

Carrel came up off his boot heels and leaned languidly against the corral, his face still calm and placid and his eyes still narrowed against the sunlight and locked with Borein's. He shrugged.

"All right, Borein. You're borrowing trouble and I'm here to see that you get it."

Carrel's voice hadn't risen but even so Borein's companion, a lesser employee of the railroad company, saw something in the build of the two men that was like granite striking flint. They were both ruthless and uncompromising and hard as nails in their own ways, and neither would surrender to the other. He cleared his throat

14

embarrassedly and forced a weak, faint grin. "Gentlemen, there must be a way we can work this out without acting like school boys." He noticed that the two men were still glaring at one another as though they hadn't heard him. He tried another tack. "Suppose we make a deal whereby the ranchers put gates in the fence and use the tracks for crossing only when they know there'll be no trains along?"

Carrel smiled softly at the speaker. "That'd be all right except for one thing. If the cattle can't get back and forth, they can't get to water."

Borein hunched his massive shoulders. He was a half a head taller than Carrel. "That's the rancher's look-out, not the railroad company's."

Carrel's smile slid off his face and the old watchful, lazy, blank look was there again. "Exactly. It's our look-out that our stock get water, and no damned railroad track's going to keep us from getting it, either."

Borein's anger returned in a rush. He glared at Carrel with a menacing gesture. "Carrel, we can bust you wide open, and, if you persist in fighting us, by God we'll do it!" Before Carrel could answer, Borein swung toward the livery rig, jerked his head savagely at his companion, and they spun out of the yard like two straight-backed ministers who had just turned up a rock and found the devil squatting there.

Carrel watched them go with a speculative

glance. An older cowboy strode up beside him and spoke with a lowered voice.

"Dammit, Kid, we don't care about their lousy fence. Take it easy. Hell, we come up here to get lost, not get shoved into the limelight."

Carrel looked at the older man's worried frown and beyond, where his other riders were milling around out of earshot. He nodded slowly.

"That's right, Sam, but, dammit, we got to make a go of this place if we're going to live like respectable folks, and that damned fence could keep us from the very thing we're after . . . respectability."

The graying cowboy nodded his grizzled head dolefully. "Well, maybe. But you be careful. They's only you an' me left now, an' all the cached loot in the world won't save us if we get into a legal tangle with no railroad company."

II

Carrel's tangle with Borein spread like wildfire. Sadler and his foreman, hulking, gaunt Sam Froman, who he'd brought with him to the Garcia holdings when he bought them, were surprised. They hadn't mentioned it to a soul. Sam asked Lem Evart, the rancher who adjoined them to the north, where he got the story. Lem sat on his wiry gray horse and scratched his ribs with enthusiasm as he answered.

16

"That's why I rode over, Sam. If they's goin' to be trouble, me an' Everett Lister want to carry our share. After all, that danged fence is our sore spot, too."

Sam frowned heavily. "Yeah, that's fine, Lem, but where did you hear about Sadler's trouble with Borein?"

Lem Evart lounged in his scuffed old saddle. "I heard it from Everett an' I believe he told me that Ruth told his girl."

Sam scratched his head in puzzlement. "Who in hell's Ruth?"

Lem laughed softly and hooked one leg around the saddle horn and reached for the makings. "Well, sir, you're still new around here, Sam. Look, Carrel an' Lister an me are the only land owners on the Estacado, right?"

Sam nodded. He knew that all right. The entire plains belonged to Evart, Lister, and Carrel, except, of course, for the railroad sections.

Lem broke his match with work-blunted fingers and sucked smoke into his lungs. "All right, now then Everett Lister's got a daughter named Betty an' she's a close friend of Borein's girl, Ruth, an' so, when Ruth told Betty about what her father told her, then of course Betty told Everett an' he told me an' now I'm tellin' you. That's simple enough, ain't it?"

Sam looked up in bewilderment. "Yeah, that's plumb simple. The only trouble is, Lem, you lost

17

me on the second curve, about two Ruths an' a Betty ago."

When the laughter had subsided, Lem Evart reiterated his intention to contribute, along with Lister and Carrel, whatever was needed to battle the railroad fence. Sam passed this information along to Carrel, when the latter got back from Isabelita.

"That's good, Sam, because I think things are about to open up."

"Yeah? How's that?"

"The boys and I found one of our imported bulls dead on the right of way."

Sam's profanity was loud, lewd, and long. "What killed him?"

"A bullet."

Sam was off again. After he had subsided a little, he became garrulous. "Damn! We paid a hell of a price for them fancy bulls. If one dies from grass poisonin', that's bad enough, but to get one shot, by God, that's murder!" His small, angry eyes drilled into Carrel. "Who done it, Kid? You got any idea?"

Sadler shrugged. "An idea, Sam, but that's all."

Sam nodded vigorously. "That's good enough for me. You jus' tell me who you figger done it an I'll. . . ."

Carrel broke out into laughter that stopped Sam in mid-sentence. "You damned fool, Sam."

"Huh?"

"Why, hell, it was only a few days ago that you were giving me hell for getting in the limelight, and now here you go, wanting to go off and salivate someone for killing a bull."

Sam scowled quickly. "Yeah, but this here is different. Our bulls cost a lot of money. They're better'n any bulls in the country. Hell, they're. . . ."

Carrel laughed again. "Hell, a man'd think you were related to 'em."

Sam saw the humor and smiled wryly. "Well, for that matter, dammit, I got kinsmen who ain't nowhere near as well-bred as them bulls are."

Carrel smiled. "All right. As long as you and the boys feel that way about it, we'll hit for Isabelita first thing in the morning and pay Borein a visit."

"You reckon he done it?"

"No, not him exactly, but I reckon he can reach out and touch the man who did."

Sam spat into his hands and rubbed them grindingly together. He was nodding grimly when he turned toward the bunkhouse. "All right, Kid. I'll see you in the mornin'."

The morning was clear and cool and the fragrance of the sage and dew-laden grass was in the nostrils of the four jogging riders who loped easily toward Isabelita. Sadler Carrel and his lean, capable-looking cowboys were astride after a full night's sleep and a rich, warm breakfast. The lightness of youth, with its fierceness and foolishness, rode with the men. All except Sam Froman were young men, but that particular day the graying Sam, caught up in the zest and verve of the younger cowboys, was just as reckless as the others.

Sadler reined up on a little bluff overlooking the straggling, wind- and sun-swept town of Isabelita. There was a long, even main street where the railroad men and the ranchers let off steam in the saloons and billiard rooms. There were also several mercantile establishments and two blacksmith shops, but, set apart, a little primly, was a clutch of better-class homes that seemed to look down on Isabelita from their slight advantage of a small hummock, with aristocratic contempt and disdain. The musical clamor of a struck anvil floated over the little town and wafted softly, gently up to the men on the bluff. Carrel shook out his reins and the four riders began the descent.

"We'll go to the depot first. Maybe we'll find Borein there, somewhere."

The shimmering twin bands of silver that ran behind the town proper were fronted by a small, yellow and brown building and a jumble of loading chutes off to the left of the depot office. The Carrel cowboys tied up at the corrals and hunkered down as Sam and Carrel walked musically into the depot office.

A railroad clerk, sitting dully beside a clicking little telegraph key, looked up idly. There was boredom and indifference on his hard face. He acknowledged Sadler's nod with an irritated frown. Sam bristled but Sadler shrugged.

"Who in hell's that penny-ante character think he is? Why, I'll. . . ."

"Aw, take it easy, Sam. You've seen enough of these railroad men to know they're all alike."

Sam grunted and eyed the clerk balefully. "Yeah, but I've a way to move 'em out of their tracks." His face lit up grimly as some recollection flitted through his mind. "Yes, sir. Usually, when I come into one of these here little coops, them railroad fellers fairly jumped up an' bowed"

Sadler's eyes wandered casually to Froman's holstered six-gun. He, too, remembered how differently some trainmen acted when they saw a gun staring owlishly at them over a counter. The clerk finally closed the clicking key and flopped back in his chair. His mildly hostile eyes flicked over the two waiting men.

"Yeah? What ya want?"

Sadler could feel Sam stiffening. He ignored the man's insulting attitude. "Borein around?"

The little, indifferent eyes squinted in contempt. "I guess you mean Mister Borein, don't you?"

That was all Sam Froman could take. With a ragged, savage oath, he reached the door leading into the clerk's bailiwick, threw it open so violently it made the whole building shake, slammed across the room, and had the railroad man by the shirt front before that startled, wide-eyed individual could get out of his chair. By furiously bulging muscles alone, Sam brought the man out of the chair. Their faces were about three inches apart when Sam spoke through clenched teeth.

"Are you tired of livin', *hombre*?"

The clerk's Adam's apple was going up and down in his throat like a squirrel in a cage. He tried twice to say something, his face an ashen white. Sam's bloodless lips pulled down, and he released the clerk and shoved at the same time. The man hit his swivel chair briefly and went over backward. Sam turned his back in contempt and strolled out of the little office, closed the door behind him, and again stood bitterly beside Carrel. He jerked his head curtly.

"Come on. Let's go find this Borein feller by ourselves."

Sam had no sooner spoken than a door opened in the wall behind the clerk's office, and Edward Borein stood frozen in the doorway. His eyes were on his disheveled, upset, and thoroughly rattled clerk who was peering around the edge of his desk cautiously and watching the cowmen. Borein's startled glance slid quickly over Carrel and Froman, then swung in amazement to his clerk.

"Sanders! What in the devil are you doing?"

The clerk looked up helplessly but Carrel spoke first. He had his gentle, disarming smile on his face and his eyes held that lazy, indifferent look. "We came in here to find you, but your man there"—he gave a toss of his head toward the gingerly arising clerk—"was a little slow in answering."

Ed Borein's big bulk was balanced on his toes for just a second as Carrel's meaning soaked in, then like a juggernaut of flesh and bone he heaved himself forward with an oath. Froman and Carrel stood across the counter as Borein slammed against it, his face livid.

"By God, Carrel, you've come into the wrong country this time. You think you're tough. Well, I'm going to see you on your knees for this outrage!"

Carrel's eyes were still cool but the faint smile had vanished. "Borein, I've come to see you about a dead bull. Know anything about it?"

The executive's eyes softened with a crafty smile of triumph. He had been angry before, but now he was bitterly elated, too, and it showed. Normally he wouldn't have been reckless in his speech, but now his caution and good sense were overruled by his fury. He ducked his head quickly in a savage nod. "You're damned right I do." The fiery eyes bored into Carrel's face. "You asked for trouble, Carrel. Now let's see how you like it."

Sam Froman snarled as he crouched, his face a mask of violence. Carrel caught Sam's steely wrist in a vise-like grip. The foreman tugged once and Carrel could feel the sinews going limp and relaxed his hold. He shook his head at Sam and turned back to Borein.

"All right, Borein. You had my bull killed for being on your tracks. That's what I figured." He nodded softly and his eyes were cold and dangerous now. "You're the one that started this, Borein, remember that the next time we meet." Under the steady, murderous glare of the railroad executive, Sadler Carrel and his foreman left the railroad office.

III

The Carrel cowboys rode up Isabelita's main street. The day was clear and warm. They tied up outside the 66 Saloon and went inside where an atmosphere of coolness swept over them. The room was almost deserted and the smell of the place was heavy with the old odors of tobacco and liquor. At the far end of the bar five men, apparently section workers for the railroad, were the sole customers before Carrel's men came in. The section hands had been drinking a lot, evidently, for their attitude was one of exultation, even that early in the day.

The cowboys ordered beer and lounged lazily against the bar as they drank. Sam Froman's face was dour. He said nothing, and Sadler Carrel, standing beside his foreman, watched Sam turn his beer glass in its sticky little ring on the bar top.

"Was the easiest bonus I ever earned." One of the section hands was speaking to his admiring companions. He was a big, massive Irishman with a slack mouth and a merry blue eye. "I jest waited till we was up close, aimed, an' fired." His big arms were up, shoulder level, holding an imaginary rifle. He ducked his head once, proudly, and let his arms drop. "The beast dropped like he'd been pole-axed."

There was an awful moment of silence. The cowboys stood rigidly while Froman and Carrel stared slowly at one another, then let their glances run the length of the bar. The section hands, oblivious to the cowmen, were smiling approvingly at their champion. Sam stepped back from the bar several steps and his legs were wide apart. "Show us how he dropped, *hombre*, when the bullet hit him."

Sam's voice hadn't raised enough to carry beyond the section workers but in an instant they heard and understood. The big Irishman looked Sam over with an initial gaze that slowly turned to uncomfortable awareness of Sam's stance.

"What's eatin' into ya, cowboy?"

Sam's face was hard and set. "I said show us, feller, and I meant it."

The big Irishman moved massively around the edge of the bar with an uneasy, lop-sided grin on his face. "I don't know what yer means, cowboy, but if it's trouble yer atter, jest lay them guns on the bar an' I'll give ye all you'll be wantin'."

Sam's shoulders drooped a little. There was no mistaking what was coming next. The Irishman hesitated, then stopped. "Mick, when I said show us how that there bull dropped, I wasn't kidding. Now you either drop like he did, or, so help me, I'll drop you myself."

The Irishman blinked a couple of times. Unarmed, he could have broken Sam Froman with his hands, but he saw from the cowman's stance that Sam had no intention of laying aside his guns. He thought for a long moment. There was no other way. The choice was simple, brief, and succinct. He shrugged, made a grimace toward his wide-eyed friends, and dropped to the sawdust-covered saloon floor. There was a long silence as the cowmen and the railroad workers looked at the red-faced corpse. Froman straightened up.

"All right, Mick. Get up." The big Irishman arose and dusted himself off. "How much did you get paid for the job?" The man's face came up and a dogged look of determination was on it. Sam shook his head and his voice was menacing. "Don't get *bravo* on me, *hombre*."

"Hunert dollars." The voice was sullen.

"Who paid you?"

"Mister Borein."

"Take your unwashed crew and clear out o'

here." The section gang left, and Sam turned to Carrel. "Well, Kid, what's the next move?"

Sadler Carrel's face was pinched. He shrugged. "I reckon it's going to be trouble for sure now, Sam." His eyes fixed themselves knowingly on the foreman's lowering features. Froman knew what Sadler meant. They'd intended to make a clean start, quit the owlhoot business, set up in the cow business, and finish out their days as respectable citizens. He shrugged slightly and shook his head.

"Yeah"—the words were soft and dry—"but if we gotta fight to keep from bein' walked on, well then, I don't reckon we got much choice, have we?"

Before Carrel could answer, a man burst into the saloon, took one long look at the cowmen lined up along the bar, turned, and ducked out again. Sam looked in surprise after the man and Carrel strode quickly toward the batwing doors, took a quick, long look outside, swore, and turned back to his men.

"That mick and about twenty men are headed this way, boys. They're carrying everything from clubs to shotguns."

The Carrel men left the bar and peered through the dingy, grimy windows down the street in the direction of the railroad siding. An unmistakable crowd of section men was fanned out across Isabelita's main street, walking slowly,

27

purposefully toward the 66 Saloon. Froman swore heartily and spun toward the bartender, who was methodically clearing his shelves and stowing the bottles under the massive bar.

"You got a back way out of this trap, pardner?"

The barkeep nodded and jerked a thumb toward a heavy oaken door on the left of the bar. Sam crossed the room, opened the door a crack, peered out, and closed and bolted it again, shaking his head. "No good, Kid. They's ten of 'em out there behind some baled hay."

Sadler Carrel was wearing a peculiar little smile as he stationed the cowboys in places of vantage. He even chuckled as he faced his foreman. "Come on, Sam. This is better'n chasing cows anyway."

Froman scratched his head ruefully. "Yeah, but I don't like this damned saloon fer a hold-out." He looked critically at the building. "Walls are like tissue paper. Hell!" He was suddenly disgusted with himself. "I should have blasted that mick when I had the chance."

Carrel shrugged and was on the point of answering when a rifle crashed and a long, jagged splinter of wood flew out of the wall over the door. The fight was on. Quickly Froman and Carrel crouched near windows and the cowmen let go their first volley. It was a flurry of shots sent out by reckless and experienced fighting men and the railroad faction quailed before its accuracy. Screams, oaths, and shouts shook Isabelita's quiet, staid business section. The town constable leaped on his horse and rode like mad for Borein's office. He ordered, pleaded, and threatened to no avail. The railroad executive was adamant. The cowmen had started a war and the railroad would see them through to the bitter end. The constable swore mightily as he rode across the wide, rolling land toward Hendrix, the county seat and sheriff's headquarters. He wasn't being paid enough to try and stop a full scale war and, anyway, he wasn't fool enough to try it alone. Let the sheriff of the county take a hand. Cursing grimly to himself, he thundered away from Isabelita and the faint thunder of popping, snarling guns sped him on his journey.

The saloon was a shambles. The bartender had disappeared and the acrid smoke lay like a gray shroud over the embattled cowmen. One of Carrel's riders had been shot through the upper arm. A bandage had been contrived that stopped the blood and the man resumed his place. Through the broken windows the Carrel faction could count four perfectly still and inert bodies lying grotesquely along Isabelita's roadway. Suddenly there was a violent fusillade of shots poured through the rear door of the saloon. The cowboys flattened themselves on the floor as the old door shook and trembled. Sam Froman swiveled his head around. His eyes were wide and concerned. He shouted over the furor to Sadler Carrel, who, hat tipped back, eyes dancing in pools of excitement, was thumbing shots into the attackers.

"Help me pile them damned tables in front of that door, Kid. If they knock it open, we're a goner."

Carrel and Froman sweated and fumed as they built their barricade. The flankers were pouring an erratic but consistent fire into the rear of the building. A bullet yanked Sam's sweaty old Stetson from his head, and he swore with feeling as he surveyed the damage. Using a knothole for a gun port, the enraged foreman poked his gun through and fired three times into the hay pile behind the saloon. The flankers were momentarily stunned by the answering fire and lay low. Sam reloaded, still eyeing the Stetson with torn crown, poked his gun through the knothole again, hunted for a target, picked a carelessly exposed boot top, and fired. A howl of pain rewarded him. There was a moment of silence, then a venomous volley of lead came his way. Sam dropped to the floor until the firing was over, arose again, sought another target, and fired again. This time two railroad men broke and ran and Sam downed both of them before they had gotten twenty feet from their barricade. At this appalling accuracy, the balance of the flankers lay low and held their fire. Sam, avenged for the ruin of his hat, returned to the front of the building and got the surprise of his life. In fact he stood still, mouth agape, and stared.

Sadler Carrel was dragging a spitting, fighting, clawing bundle of something inside the saloon window. Apparently he had found the attacker just below the sill trying to get into a position to throw something into the saloon. Holstering his gun, Sam rushed up to help. As he did so, Carrel released the howling dervish and leaped wildly backward just in time to miss a wild, furious swing that whistled past his face.

Sam's hurtling form struck the wild-eyed, disheveled attacker like a battering ram and they went to the floor together. Carrel rushed forward to help just as Sam's face, bleeding from four livid scratch marks, emerged from the threshing turmoil with a look of incredulity and horror on it. He pushed away from the furious attack of the smaller man and leaped to his feet. He faced Carrel, ran a grimy paw to the bloody gashes on his face, and there was a stupid look of disbelief on his face.

"It ain't no man, Kid. It's a. . . ."

The kick caught Sam in the shins and he bellowed out a wild curse and grasped his wounded appendage and hopped crazily out of range. Carrel picked up his hat, blocked it slowly, and plunked it on his head.

"Come on, wildcat, cut it out. We ain't fighting you no more. Calm down."

The ragged, dirty, pug-nosed fighter came off the floor, chest heaving and eyes red. Sam limped

31

up and poked an accusing finger at the stranger.

"You got no right to go around kickin' folks. Why, fer two cents I'd. . . ." He chopped it off suddenly and hobbled hastily backward as the smaller man began to take his weight off his booted toe. "Uh, uh, no more o' that."

Carrel's faint grin was back. "Who are you?"

"None of your business." The voice clinched it. The invader wasn't a man at all. It was a girl.

IV

Sam nodded his head and looked helplessly at Carrel. "I knew it, Kid, when I was wrestlin' with him . . . er . . . her."

Carrel's eyes twinkled and the girl's blazing eyes snapped when she faced Sam.

"You shut up!" Sam held his respectful distance and looked from the furious girl to his boss. Carrel felt like laughing. She was so small, so obviously female, and so pretty, with her smudged face, flashing white teeth, and fiery eyes.

"Please ma'am, I don't know why you wanted to throw that there stink bomb in here, unless you're the wife of one of those unwashed section laborers, and let's just quit fightin' for a minute, will you?"

"I'm not a section laborer's wife. I'm Ruth Borein. And if you think you cowmen run this country, you're going to find out differently now.

You've been riding rough-shod over the railroad long enough and my father's going to make you eat crow." She shook the mass of her taffy-colored hair and stamped her foot. "You've started something this time, Mister Cowman, that the railroad'll finish!" Suddenly she stopped her harangue and her eyes widened. She thought back to the moment Sadler Carrel had stood bareheaded, punching his hat back into shape, and her face blanched a little. She stared at him hard for a long moment before she spoke again, and then her voice was small. "I know who you are."

Froman stiffened and Carrel looked up quickly. The smile was gone now. "Who?"

"The Gila River Kid."

For a long second the thundering, ear-splitting crash of guns wasn't heard by the trio as their eyes locked. Carrel was the first to speak. "What makes you think so?"

Ruth Borein pointed a small hand at Carrel's head. "When you lost your hat dragging me through the window, I saw the crescent scar." Her hand dropped limply to her side. "In my father's office there's a description of you and it tells about the scar. You got it in a train robbery over in New Mexico. It's all the law has to go on. No pictures, just that crescent scar."

The girl was biting her lip now. There was fear in the eyes that only a moment before had been full of defiance. She watched Sadler Carrel with a sort of wide-eyed hypnotic stare. He looked slowly at Sam Froman and the foreman's frown proved the jig was up. He swung back to the girl.

"I'm sorry, Miss Borein, but we'll have to tie you up."

Ruth Borein was silent while she was tied to a chair behind the bar. Her gaze seldom left Carrel's face, and, although he avoided looking at her, he was acutely conscious of her intent study of him. He arose and stood over the prisoner, looking gravely down. Froman dashed toward the front of the gutted saloon when a swell of yelling rose over the rattle of gunfire.

"Miss Borein, every man makes mistakes. I've made plenty. Maybe buying the old Garcia place and trying to settle down and become a respectable cattleman was the biggest." The broad shoulders rose and fell. "Anyway, I've enjoyed my brief life as a decent rancher." The faint smile flickered around the corners of his mouth again. "Well, you've pretty well busted all that for me now, so, as soon as Sam and I can get out of here, we'll slip away with my riders and get out of the country, and your father can say he beat us." The grin was being forced now. "I'm sorry you recognized me, Miss Borein, but I reckon that's fate, isn't it?"

Ruth Borein's violet eyes held Carrel's glance. She swallowed once with an effort. "I don't know what to say. It's all too confusing." She dropped her eyes, but, as Carrel turned away, they flashed back up and ran quickly over his broad-shouldered, narrow-hipped form.

The railroaders were staying out of sight. They weren't any match for the embattled cowboys and had found it out at no little cost. Big Ed Borein alone showed himself as he went from barricade to barricade talking, gauging, and directing the assault on the saloon. At Carrel's orders he was spared when, a number of times, he could have been killed. Froman looked strangely at the Kid when he ordered his men to leave the railroad executive alone. Carrel shrugged.

"Hell, Sam, killing her old man won't make it any better."

The foreman started to speak but looked closely at the Kid, shrugged, and turned back to his bullet-pocked window without saying a word. Carrel's sober eyes rested for a long time on Froman's back. Sam had wanted to be respectable for so long. They had sat at the rendezvous many a starlit night and talked and planned with such high hopes, and here they were, again, hunted and hounded, and worse—as soon as possible they had to hit out for the dim, narrow, and crooked trails of the owlhoot world. The Gila River Kid felt a pang of sadness flash through him. Sam had an orphaned niece somewhere, living in the Middle West with relatives, that he doted on. He'd talked of bringing her to live with him someday, when he had hung up his guns. The Kid turned away with a smothered oath.

The fight was almost a stalemate. The firing had dropped to a sporadic, almost indifferent exchange by men whose first passion had subsided. The railroad men were hidden. Those who had been careless, once, no longer fired. The cowboys were pressed for targets, weary and almost out of ammunition. The Kid had found a carbine and several boxes of shells behind the bar, on one of his trips back there, and with these the defenders felt a little better, although they were still a long way from being cheered. Two of Carrel's men had been hit. One was shot through the mouth. The bullet hadn't even hit a tooth, but it had plowed through the cheek and left a purplish, rapidly swelling wound that was nasty-looking. The other wounded man was the young rider who'd been hit in the upper arm in the first exchange of lead.

In one of the intermittent lulls in the battle, Borein showed himself. He stood, wide-legged, facing the saloon. A .30-30 carbine dangled from his massive paws.

"You, in there!"

The Kid held up a hand and his men held their fire. "Yeah, Borein, what d'ya want?"

"You got my daughter?"

"Yeah. She's safe enough."

"She hurt any?"

"No. But only a damned fool would let a girl try a stunt like that."

Borein's voice was anxious and edgy. "I didn't know she was out of the house." He was quiet for a second. "Let her out, will you?"

The Kid looked at Sam. The older man nodded his head slowly. The Kid smiled gratefully. "All right, Borein, we'll turn her loose on one condition."

"What is it?"

"You have your men bring our horses up to the front of the saloon and hold their fire until we're out of town."

Two men approached Borein as he started to answer. He swung to hear them. The Kid and his men could see them pointing out over the range behind them. They were arguing vehemently, but Borein shook his head doggedly and swung back toward the saloon.

"All right, Carrel, we'll bring your horses and give you a clean bill of health until you're out of town."

The Kid turned to his men as Borein's men began to show themselves and several scuttled after the cowmen's horses. "Don't shoot, boys. We'll get out of this hornet's nest and try to make it back to the ranch, where we can get help in case they come after us."

Froman got slowly to his feet. "They'll be after us, you can bet on that." He jerked his head toward the townsmen. "They can see something coming across the range. Probably the sheriff an' a posse from Hendrix."

The Kid turned away and walked behind the bar. For a long moment he fumbled in his pocket for his knife. "Miss Borein, I reckon you heard us yelling back and forth?" She nodded as he knelt down and began cutting the rope bounds. "Well, good luck and . . ."—he was blushing furiously now—"I sort of wish things had been a little different. I mean, I wish we weren't on opposite sides." The ropes fell off her and she sat very still, looking at him.

"I thought outlaws were all killers."

The Kid's smile bobbed up and his eyes twinkled. "That's too long a story to take up here, ma'am. Someday, maybe, I'll get a chance to explain it to you." He helped her up. "Ruth"—he blushed again, but he had wanted to call her that—"promise me something, will you?" She nodded calmly, grave-eyed. "Don't ever pull a stunt like you did today again. The graveyards are full of folks that get reckless and I'd sure hate to think you'd be one of 'em." He turned away as he spoke and didn't see the small, capable hand move up, as though to stop him and the full, generous mouth open a little. "Come on," he said over his shoulder, "the horses are here."

V

Ruth Borein walked out of the devastated 66 Saloon. She was a little stiff and there were several smudges of dirt on her face, but aside from that she appeared healthy enough. Her anxious father threw a warm arm around her sturdy shoulders as she came up to him.

"Honey, I ought to spank you, but I'm so darned glad to see you alive, I'm weak all over." He threw a grim, lowering glare over his shoulder at the stiffly mounting, wary cowboys. "Was it pretty awful?"

For the first time Ruth looked up and spoke. Her gaze went slowly, irresistibly to the straight-backed, tense riders, jogging down the main street of Isabelita toward the range beyond. She was so intent in watching one figure that she didn't sense the hysterical stillness, the deathly, awful tenseness that had settled down over the little town.

"No, Dad. It wasn't awful." Ruth was standing there, very sober and small, beside her gray-eyed father, watching the exodus from Isabelita. A rifle poked out of an upper window in the old hotel, followed the retreating riders like a black, avenging finger, then erupted venomously with a noise that echoed and reëchoed across the still, silent reaches and broke the deathly quiet with its treacherous shout that meant it was no respecter of truces. The Gila River Kid sagged, struggled hard to regain his seat, slumped unconsciously, and dropped soddenly to the dusty, hard roadway. For a long moment there was absolute silence. The riders reined up and sat stupified, looking down at their bleeding leader. Sam Froman swung down and knelt by the Kid. In a flash he was on his feet, a snarling, savage oath erupting from down deep in his barrel chest. He whirled on the frozen townsmen, rooted, as they were, by the suddenness of the treachery in their midst. His gun leaped out of its holster, and in the clearness of the silence everyone heard the hammer click back. Borein shook out of his amazed horror.

"Hold it. Don't anybody move. Claude, Jim, Bob, get the man that fired that shot if you have to kill him to do it." He waved a big arm toward the hotel, where a smallish cloud of blue smoke was still lazily floating over the assassin's window. Ed Borein was rigid. He knew that anything, now, could cause the entire fight to reërupt into bloody savagery and he meant to keep that from happening. He elbowed past Ruth and began to walk slowly, evenly toward the cowmen. Froman's cocked gun was belly high and the foreman's eyes were deadly. Borein spoke lowly.

"Don't do it, cowboy. Don't pull that trigger.

Whoever fired that shot will be caught. It was a low-down, sneaky act and whoever did it'll pay the full cost, believe me. But if you pull that trigger, all hell'll break loose again." Borein and Froman were close enough now to face each other over the ugly snout of Sam's .45. With another curse, Sam holstered his gun and swung abruptly away from the railroad executive and knelt again beside his employer.

Sam's bandanna, limp and red with the Kid's blood, was held in his clenched fist when Ed Borein knelt beside the two men. Neither was conscious of the small, roguish little figure that pushed in between them until two small, strong hands went out tenderly and wiped the welling blood out of the victim's eyes, then they looked. Ruth's face was ashen and her lips were trembling. Sam looked over her tousled head toward her father as he gently relinquished the Gila River Kid's upper body and the small, sturdy little nurse took over.

Sam swore under his breath when he looked at the ragged slit over the wounded man's ear where the bullet had narrowly missed penetrating his skull. "The second time in the same place." He was shaking his head when Borein, frowning in puzzlement, looked at him.

"What d'ya mean?"

Sam looked up suddenly and scowled guiltily. "Nothin', not a damned thing."

Borein was still watching Sam when his men came running up. He turned to face them. "Did you get the bushwackin' scum?"

"No, sir. He run past us, clambered on a horse, an' lit out," one of them said.

Sam let out a savage whoop and leaped for his horse. "Come on, boys, they's work to be done." As he whirled away, he looked back at Ruth Borein. "You'll guard over him, won't you, ma'am?"

Ruth looked up and Sam noticed the mistiness in her eyes. Before she could answer, the grizzled outlaw touched his hat brim briefly with a massive hand and made a slight, old-fashioned bow, then he was gone with his wild, wrathful riders thundering along in his wake like some of hell's imps astride.

It was late before the Kid opened his eyes. There was a lamp hissing and sputtering on a broad old oaken table with great dragon-footed legs. The Kid closed his eyes quickly. The light hurt. He opened them a squinting bit and fascination showed in his face. Fascination and amazement, because he was in a strange room, with curtains at the windows and pastel colors on the chairs and in the filmy things he saw. With an effort that cost a little pain, the Kid rolled his head gently to one side and got another shock. His eyes literally fell into the anxious stare of a small, sturdy, big-eyed little angel with full red mouth and a small pug nose. The Kid grinned weakly.

"Ruth, if you're real, you sure are a lot cleaner than the last time we met."

Ruth made a wry face and smiled in vast relief. "Oh, I'm so glad you're all right."

"Honest, Ruth, this isn't a dream?"

She colored a little and walked over and stood at the side of his bed. "It's no dream, Kid. I'm real. One of the railroad men shot you as you were leaving Isabelita. Your men are hunting for him."

"But where am I?"

"In our house. In my bed, in fact." Again that small tinge of color crept into the creamy cheeks.

"But Ruth, your father'll raise the devil if he finds me here." Carrel started to raise up, and Ruth's hands were flat against his chest as she pushed him gently back.

"Don't be silly. Dad wanted to bring you here. He's awfully sorry one of his men broke the parole and shot you."

The Kid looked down at the small strong hands on his chest; slowly he brought his own bronzed paws up over the counterpane and covered Ruth's hands. He looked up soberly almost lugubriously in his anxiety.

"Ruth?"

"Yes?"

"Uh . . . say . . . uh . . . how badly shot am I?"

Ruth pulled her hands away and straightened up

43

slowly with disappointment plain on her face. "You're awfully lucky, Kid. The bullet plowed a nasty furrow just over your left ear. An inch closer and it would have killed you."

"My left ear?"

Ruth nodded slowly. She understood and smiled. "Kid, when that wound heals, it'll completely cover the crescent scar. Nobody will ever know you were the Gila River Kid, if you don't want them to, or . . ."—she hesitated—"if you don't go back to the owlhoot trail."

For a moment their eyes held, then the full significance of his luck soaked in and the Kid grunted softly. "Well, then, Ruth, it's safe to say what I started to say a minute ago. Will you marry me?"

Ruth's eyes were misty again and her round chin quivered once. She didn't trust her voice, so she nodded, and, as she did, the bedroom door burst open and Sam Froman, sweat-streaked, dusty, and red-eyed, strode into the room with Ed Borein beside him. Both men were grinning from ear to ear. Sam yanked up a frail little chair, dropped his torn Stetson on the floor, and sank his big bulk onto the chair, completely hiding it's dainty framework.

"Kid, me an' Borein here's been outside that danged door for near fifteen minutes waitin' fer you to get up guts enough to say it." He shook his head doggedly. The Kid looked anxiously from one of the older men to the other. Ruth's softness fled and in its place was the old fire. She pulled herself up to her full five feet and one inch and her eyes flashed fire.

"You bullies leave him alone. He's a sick man."

Sam got up hastily and pushed the little chair in front of him. "Now, now, ma'am, don't go an' get sore." He turned to the Kid. "Watch 'er, *hombre*, she kicks like a mule."

The Kid was strangling an urge to laugh when he spoke. "Where's the snake that plugged me, Sam?"

Sam, still keeping an eye on the diminutive girl, rubbed a plainly thoughtful hand over his blunt jaw. "Dang, it, Kid, that there bushwhacker gave us one hell . . . uh, pardon me, ma'am . . . of a chase but we finally got him cornered in a little cañon and he took up a tree like a monkey." Sam shook his head in sad recollection. "We like to never got him out, either, till one o' the boys roped him an' commenced to pull him down."

Borein, who was following Sam's story with great interest, frowned. "He didn't get away, did he?"

Sam shook his head slowly. "No, not exactly, but you know what happened? Why, danged if that there lariat didn't get all tangled up in the tree and the poor feller's still hangin' there." Sam looked so doleful the others didn't catch on for a moment, then they all began to laugh, and, when

45

the noise had died down a little, Ruth looked at her father.

"Dad, besides paying the Kid for his dead bull, I have a swell idea."

Ed Borein squirmed once, then looked resigned. "What is it?"

"Instead of cutting the cowmen off from their other range, across the tracks, you could dig under passes and the cattle could go back and forth as they pleased."

Ruth's idea was new and its merit took a little time to appreciate. The men looked blankly at one another for a while, then Sam Froman slapped his leg sharply. "That's the best danged thing I ever heard of. How about you, Sadler?"

The Kid looked hungrily at the mite of woman by his bed. "It takes brains to think up something like that, Sam, real brains."

Ed Borein scratched his head slowly and studied his daughter. "Hey, wait a minute. Dang it, it's bad enough to lose my only daughter to a cowman, but darned if she isn't beginning to think like a cowman already, and it's going to cost the railroad money." He sighed and laughed. "That's all right, though. I know when I'm whipped." He winked at Carrel, who returned the wink owlishly.

The Man Without a Gun

I

"Swift," the warden said, pushing his words out loudly and sharply, "you've tamed down considerable since you first came here. For a while we had two men watching you. I'm glad you got hold of yourself. I hate spies as much as the prisoners do, but in here we've got to have them."

The warden swung his head toward a window. "See out there? Those headboards? Well, they didn't all die of yellow jack. A lot of them didn't know about our inside spy system. When a prisoner tries to escape from Yuma Prison, the chances are his escape will be permanent."

The warden returned his attention to the silent man across the desk from him. Some of the harshness left his voice. "Forget all that," he went on. "It's behind you. Just a couple more minutes and you can go. You've paid for what you were sent here for . . . horse stealing. I'm glad, Swift. You don't have to believe that and I don't give a damn whether you do or not . . . but I'm glad every time a man walks out of here. The only time I'm off them is when they return. Remember that, Swift. Don't come back.

"Now then, you don't want any advice, but you're going to get it anyway. First off . . . if you made any friends in here, forget them. Secondly, if you've got old friends outside, forget them, too. Break clean, Swift, and start over fresh. You're a single man and you're free, so don't go back where you got into trouble. Going back's never any good, anyway.

"For a while it'll be hard on you. Don't make it any harder by being bitter and vengeful. You had seventeen dollars when you came here three years ago . . . there it is. The gun you'll never get back and from now on it's against the law for you to own one. Remember that, Swift. Don't pack a gun."

For a silent moment the warden gazed steadily at the unmoving big man, then he leaned forward and extended a hand.

"Good bye and good luck."

It was seven miles to the first town, a long walk back. The sun overhead was a malevolent orange disc, and the dust that arose after each step was bitterly alkaline.

Even for a young man the sudden mantle of freedom after three years of restriction was not an easy thing to adjust to. He was alone and adrift, a stranger to this big world of summer, and also a stranger to himself. He wouldn't go back, no, but where would he go? What would he do?

He moved through the waves of heat scuffling dust in too-tight boots. His arms swung easily in the shrunken shirt. Free. And while heat made a smear of distance, he thought back, his mind a gray mixture of strangeness with little threads of sorrow tangled in its workings.

He had been an overgrown kid at twenty-seven. Now, at thirty, he was a full-fledged man. Three years had forced a late maturing. Better to mature late than not to mature at all.

Walking down the empty shimmering road he thought back and let the grayness run on. Nothing. No horse, no saddle, no gun. Yet, there was something—a felon's stain. Ex-convict Jack Swift. Something else, too. Freedom.

He trudged along, swinging his body and feeling the freedom, knowing the deep-down richness of it. It had taken him three years to learn exactly what freedom was. But he would never forget, not now—not ever again. For a range-bred man confinement was a sort of death. Not until he had survived three years of it did he understand what freedom meant. You felt no humbleness, no appreciation of freedom—until you lost it.

Then, in the first town he came to, striding through the alternate heat and shade, mingling with other free people, he saw their knowing looks, heard the sly comments and felt color rise in his cheeks.

But he cherished this freedom too much to react as he once would have; he did not turn, plant his legs wide, and roar a challenge. Instead, he continued to walk until each heel had a blister and his feet steamed like boiled beef, and his hatless head grew light inside, and his vision blurred. Walked until the miles flowed together in molten monotony and finally stopped when evening came, seeking the stage station in another town. He held up some limp bills and asked for a ticket.

The clerk looked at him in long silence before he said: "Sure, mister, but where to? You got to have a destination."

And then the echoes: *Don't go back. Break clean. Start over fresh. Going back never did any good, anyway. . . .*

"Some place where there's shade," he said to the curious face before him. "Shade and maybe a creek, open country, good grass. You know where there's such a place?"

The clerk's lips quirked. He made a sad little joke. "Yeah. Heaven." The words died and the clerk looked uncomfortable. "Hard to find anything like that in Arizona, mister." He was thoughtful for a moment, then added: "You ever been to Herd? It's three days' ride from here. Off the main trails a few miles. It's got trees and even a creek."

The big man pushed his money forward. "To Herd," he said, and that was how he came to arrive in Herd, Arizona Territory, the blistering summer of 1872, when the sun hung, iron-red and low, beyond ranks of marching mountains and the range ran like a frozen ocean out into eternity, flat as the palm of his hand.

He slept the first night in the tangled thickets along the creek bottom, then in the morning he went into the town, bought a new shirt, Levi's, boots, and had a gigantic breakfast at a hash house. After that the lemon-yellow sun looked different. Even the dust and timelessness of the desert seemed different, seemed friendly.

A little silver remained in his pocket but the paper money was gone. He went down by the community water trough and sat in the shade there. Riders passed; people who were not ex-felons nodded. He heard the quicksilver call of boys, the barking of dogs, things he had forgotten existed. Then, when the hour was right and the morning rush was over, the clean-up and wash-down period began. He crossed the roadway to the livery barn.

The liveryman was small, aged beyond reckoning, with once-blue eyes now faded to a rheumy white, and a pair of incongruously bowed legs. He greeted the big man with a quick appraisal and a short nod.

"I was wondering if you needed any help?"

The old eyes made a slower appraisal; they took in the wide sweep of chest, the thickness of big shoulders, the red and peeling face. They did not miss the unmoving eyes or the haunted shadows in their depths.

"Ever work in a livery barn before?"

"No. But I've been a horseman all my life."

"Cowboy?"

"Cowboy, horse-breaker, blacksmith, saddle. . . ."

"Come along with me."

The old man started down the wide alleyway flanked by tie and box stalls. When he halted with an arm up and pointing, he said: "Nice critter, ain't she?"

The big man leaned on the half door, gazing in. The mare was nice. She was big, seal-brown in color, docile-looking with a stud neck, and well fleshed-out.

"She's nice," he agreed.

"What's wrong with her?"

The mare was pointing. Swift sought other faults and found none.

"Sore feet," he said.

The liveryman pursed his lips. "Could a good smith fix that, young feller?"

"Yes."

"How?"

There was a quiet smile in the big man's eyes when he faced around. "With spreaders. Pine tar and leather pads. Change shoes every three, four weeks and add more spread. It's contraction . . . not very serious."

"Hot shoes?"

The quiet smile broadened. "I never saw spreaders made from cold shoes."

The old man's shrewd look altered. He, too, smiled, his face breaking up into lines and wrinkles like erosion scores. "What's your name, big feller?"

"Jack Swift."

"Mine's Buck. Andrew Jackson Buck. When do you want to start?"

"Can I bunk here?"

"Sure. In the loft if you don't smoke . . . in the harness room if you do. Tomorrow morning?"

"Fine."

"You got enough to eat on till then?"

"Yes."

Buck turned away. "Then I'll see you in the morning."

Swift went back out into the sunshine. Across the road a wagon seat was bolted to a big sycamore tree. He went there, sat down, made a cigarette, and let a feeling of looseness, of belonging somewhere, run through him.

The tobacco smoke hung lazily, blue-gray in the air. People passed. Time spun out. It was good to belong. A thought struck him and he smiled. He had forgotten to ask about his wages.

A man as big as Jack Swift strolled by. He was much older, though, and grizzled. A lawman's star hung from his shirt front. He nodded. Jack nodded back—with a solid weight lying in the pit of his stomach.

II

Those first days passed pleasantly. It was good to shoe horses, to harness them, and ache a little from hard labor. It was good to live in the easy world of horsemen again, to laze in the cool alleyway, to talk with old Buck when they waited out the dead hours. It was good to belong.

And later, when kids began hanging around, he enjoyed their company, too. Listening to them he learned names, relationships, feuds of the town, learned more about Herd in a few days from the kids than he'd have learned about it in years from their parents.

He discovered something else, too, something he'd never thought of before. That boys were sharply observant, knew a lot without trying to know any of it, were wise without seeming to be, and seethed with information without caring that they did.

One blistering hot day, when the boys did not appear and Jack was filling in the hours with saddle and harness maintenance, a solitary lad came into the barn from the back alley. He walked oddly, with one foot crooked inward, with a hesitant step, a vague limp. Watching him come forward, the big man thought he had the bluest eyes he had ever seen.

The lad stood motionlessly in the shadows,

watching Jack dismantle a saddle, oil the undersides of leather with the saddle maker's elixir—half neat's-foot oil, half mutton tallow, heated and applied with a paintbrush—and he said nothing, but his blue eyes followed each brush stroke.

Jack laid out the skirts, rosaderos, stirrup leathers and jockeys, flesh side up, and dipped the brush into the pan. "Pretty hot out," he said.

"Yes."

"Don't believe I've seen you around before."

"No," the boy replied. "I just came over today. Heard the fellers were hanging around here now. My name's Logan. They call me Rob."

Jack made a long stroke and watched the oil glisten briefly, then disappear. "Rob? Is your first name Robert?"

"Yes."

"How come folks don't call you Bob?"

The thin face remained expressionless. Only the eyes moved. "My mother called me Rob, so everyone else does."

The boy, encouraged by Jack's friendliness, shuffled closer. The big man looked down and around. There were drag marks in the dust and the small face held more years than youth should know. He saw something else there, too, a reflection of deep knowledge locked away from the rest of the world. He could recognize that expression because he also had it. He resumed his work.

"How come you aren't down at the creek fishing?"

The boy looked up quickly. "Is that where the fellers went today?"

"Yeah."

"They didn't tell me."

Jack's gaze went back to the thin face. He said—"Oh."—and the brush resumed its long, even strokes.

Kids were cruel like Indians—senselessly cruel. What the hell's a limp? Lots of folks had them. He could remember a man who had limped; he could remember him vividly.

"Can I help, mister?"

"Sure, glad to have you."

He wiped the brush handle off, slanted it in the pan, and looked into the blue eyes. "Tell you how we'll work it, Rob. I'll take them apart and you oil 'em. All right?"

Robert Logan moved forward. His shoulders hunched from the effort and his right leg dragged in the dust. Jack turned quickly away, reaching for another saddle. He spoke while his back was turned, grabbing the first words that came along.

"Don't you like to fish, Rob?"

"Well . . . yes."

"You don't sound like you do."

"I do, only I don't know the good fishing holes." Rob took up the brush and made a long sweep with it over a curling saddle skirt.

"Why not?"

"It's rocky along the creek. I got to be careful in loose rock."

Jack worked over the next saddle, worked loose the strings that were double-spliced in front of leather conchos. He heard meaning without trying to and saw painful hurt without looking for it. He knew there were beads of sweat on the thin face, felt motion where thin arms worked and tough young tendons moved.

"You live in town, Rob?"

"The last house north, just on the outskirts. I live with my grandfather. My dad used to drive the Bartlesville stage . . . from here to there. He got killed in a flash flood in Muerto Cañon when I was real little."

"Oh."

"And my mother died, too. She got sick last fall. . . ."

Jack reached for the initiative in this conversation. He spread words around and forged them into loose meaning, drawing upon things he was familiar with while he worked on the saddle, tugged off skirts, stirrup leathers, peeled back the seating leather and made it fast with strings behind the cantle.

Rob Logan asked questions, about saddles, about horses, about places and people, and finally stopped oiling to gaze solemnly at the big man when he answered. Finally he said: "You sure know a lot, mister."

Jack knew then that he had overshot his mark. Instead of taking the boy's mind off unpleasantness he'd aroused his curiosity. "No," he said. "I don't know very much, Rob."

"Saddles, horses, cowboying." The blue eyes had lost their dullness. "Mister, did you ever know any outlaws?"

The big hands fumbled. "Well, now, Rob, nobody wants to know outlaws."

"Well. You've known lawmen, haven't you?"

"I've known a few lawmen, yes."

"Then you must've known outlaws, too. Maybe not known them exactly, but seen them anyway."

Seen outlaws, known outlaws? Like Jack Britton—who also had a limp—and the Calabasas Kid—Red Ewart, Tex Connelly, and Jack Swift of old Tularosa. Gunfighters, horse thieves, hard drinkers, night riders. . . .

"Haven't you, mister?"

"Just call me Jack."

"Haven't you, Jack?"

"I reckon I've seen my share of outlaws," the big man said, looking pointedly at the motionless brush. "You've got to get that oil on before it cools, Rob. If it gets too thick, we'll have to heat it again."

The thin arm dipped, stroked up and down, and a lock of russet hair tumbled over the boy's thin forehead.

"Jack?"

60

"Huh?"

"Did you ever know an outlaw that limped?"

Swift's hands grew still among the leathers. "Why?"

"I limp. Sometimes I hate it bad enough to be an outlaw."

The big man raised up and turned very slowly. There was something you said to a kid at a time like this—what was it? What the warden had said at Yuma? No, that came afterward—three years afterward.

He began to make a cigarette. Folded it carefully, firmed it up, and lit it. Watching the even, gentle brush strokes, he said: "That's no way to talk, Rob." It wasn't what he wanted to say and it sounded totally inadequate, but it was all he could think of just then.

The blue eyes jumped to his face. "Not for you. You're big and you don't limp. I can't even fight good. Bet you can, can't you?"

"What'll fighting get you, Rob?"

But the blue eyes were glowingly measuring the great depth of chest, the powerful width of shoulders, and the mightily massive arms of the big man.

"That's why you don't wear a gun, isn't it? Because you don't need one. You lick 'em with your hands."

"That oil's. . . ."

"I wish I could do that someday. Fight real good."

"You're still a kid."

"No one'd call me limpy then."

Jack smoked and watched the thin face. Somehow this conversation had gotten entirely away from him.

"I'd like to be a marshal, too, only who'd hire a limpy marshal?"

Jack's gaze dropped to the warped leg. "How'd it happen, Rob?"

"Right after my paw was killed, when I was little, I ran after a puppy when the freighters were going through."

"Wheels went over your leg?"

"Yes."

Jack's glance returned to the pan. "You'd better hurry or we'll have to heat that stuff again."

They worked through the rich saffron shadows of afternoon and abruptly Rob said: "Did you ever feel like that . . . like you'd like to learn to use a gun real good so's folks'd be scairt of you?"

Jack was arranging the pieces to be oiled. "Listen," he said shortly, "I don't reckon there was ever a man who didn't have troubles, but most men carry them without turning mean about them. Now take you. Wouldn't it have been a heap worse if you'd gotten both legs busted . . . or maybe your backbone crushed? With a busted backbone you don't get around at all. See what I mean?"

The blue eyes looked up with a hard wisdom.

"That's what my grandpa says. But I'm still a limpy and nobody likes to play with me."

Blue eyes looked into gray eyes, words dwindled, and Rob went back to work. For a long time he was silent, then he said: "Maybe I could learn to be a saddle maker. I'd rather be a bronco buster, but that hurts too much, doesn't it? I'd better be a saddle maker."

Jack took up another saddle without answering and slammed it down on the workbench. He went to work on it with angry fingers. *Fear's in this kid, fear of pain because he's had his share of it.* When you talked to a kid like this, you had to be careful.

"Saddle makers make good money," he said. "Maybe someday you'd own your own shop. Like doctors, Rob, there's never enough good saddle makers."

The boy turned and watched Jack's hands as they disassembled the saddle with unhesitating confidence. "You know saddles real well, don't you?"

"I've been around them in one way or another all my life, Rob."

"Teach me what you know about them . . . and horse breaking . . . and cowboying." Rob sucked in a big breath and said with fierce intensity: "And teach me how to fight, Jack."

"If you learn all there is to know about saddles, it'll take most of your time, Rob. All fighting'll do is land you in a heap of trouble."

The afternoon waned, its silence broken now and then by words between the man and the boy. Pieces of leather hung from a wire over a tub for excess oil to drip into. Then, when the shadows came, Rob Logan left. The big man watched him depart, dragging his crooked leg.

"Jack?" Buck came bowlegging his way down the evening.

"Yes."

"Wasn't that the Logan kid back here with you?"

"Yes."

"Well," Buck said, small eyes lingering on the rows of hanging leather darkly rich with oil, "a feller's got to watch out for kids around a barn."

"I watch them, Buck."

"I know you do. But a man's got to watch like a hawk. They can get hurt dozens of ways a grown man'd never think of getting it." Buck dug out a big silver watch and squinted at it. "I'm going home. Light the coach lamps out front, will you? See you tomorrow."

"Good night," Jack said.

Evening descended. There was feeding to do, cleaning up, some patrolling among the squealing animals in the outside corral. A little livery business, too, among young bucks who wanted to rent top buggies with lap robes, but finally there was stillness, a leavening of the long, dying day, a period of hush and twilight and peacefulness.

That was when memories came crowding up.

Jack stood out back and smoked. Night shadows hid the cast-off horseshoes, the heat-shriveled hoof parings, and overhead the moon, disheveled and slovenly, rode serenely among her spoiled offspring—stars—lonely and a million miles away.

He thought of Rob Logan's deformity. The thin face haunted him, its vivid intensity forcing a realization that hurt made of people what otherwise they would not be. A withered arm, an ugly face, a dragging leg, a sense of apartness, a fear that life was casting them upon a stage for others to pity and to scorn.

For the first time in his life he understood with easy clarity why a man named Britton, who also limped, was more savage than an Indian when he was drunk. Jack Britton, one of the fastest and deadliest gunmen in the whole Southwest. Also known as the Sundance Kid.

He turned finally, his cigarette burned out, and strolled up through the barn past feeding horses, and lit the carriage lamps that hung high on either side of the barn's roadside entrance. Then he went down to the harness room where his cot was.

Being alone like this at the end of the day was an old familiar ache. He felt the sadness, the loneliness more than ever. It spread upward and outward, bringing him down to a bitter sense of personal futility. Then daylight came again and life was once again bearable.

The hot, golden days flowed outward toward an early fall with the fragrance of coming rain in it. And Jack's limping, wistful shadow was never far off. There were questions and looks and longings in Rob's blue eyes. He and the big man became close. Then an old gelding named Johnny Reb developed distemper, something usually associated with much younger animals. Buck was away, something to do with an Army cartage contract.

Johnny Reb was an unhandsome old Grulla horse, but gentle with a rare, philosophical quietude. They put him in a pleasant stall and fed him warm rolled barley mash, timothy hay, and waited for the glands under his jaw to swell. Jack explained how this happened, and, when Rob came eagerly one morning to tell him there was a big swelling, he and the lad went to the stall together. There, Jack took out his pocket knife and talked as he honed it.

Rob stared at that knife until he could no longer stand the silver reflection of it and a shudder passed over him.

"You've got to learn these things," Jack was saying. "Because, whether we like to do them or not, they've got to be done. See here, see how gray and pulpy that swelling is. See how the hair's slipped. Feel up here . . . that soft spot."

"Yes."

"That's where it's headed up."

"Are you going to cut it there?"

A nod. "Drain it. If we don't, it'll cut off his air."

"But it's not near his nose, Jack."

"No, it's under his throat here. That's where the air goes into his lungs."

Johnny Reb's big dark eyes watched them listlessly. They were dry-hot and tired old eyes.

There was a sound of ripping flesh, a gush of ill-smelling poison—and Rob fled, leg dragging, leaving squiggly marks in the alleyway and sounds of soft swiftness.

Outside, beyond the barn, the sun was pale. The grass beyond town was cured into drabness and the world shimmered evilly around the boy. Closed in oppressively, then danced outward. He walked along with sticky dust underfoot. He was completely alone until he emerged from a dirty dogtrot between two buildings that was rank with urine scent, and stood upon the plank walk of Herd's main thoroughfare. Down a way he saw a fine buggy draw up before a house, saw a woman get down, turn, and smile at the man who had driven her home.

Her hair was short, burnished where the light struck it. When she moved, it was with grace, like she was floating. Rob watched her without moving a muscle. She would be like that. His mother.

Then the buggy drove off, the woman disappeared indoors, and emptiness returned.

67

He walked as far as the water trough and sank down upon the buggy seat there that was bolted to a big sycamore tree.

Then the anguish hit him. Hard, solidly, like a fist. It made his throat constrict and his eyes blur.

He remembered the terror of that night when people had come to his grandfather's house. Solemn-faced people, looking a little over his head or avoiding his eyes. The night his mother died. He remembered his grandfather trying to explain, how he refused to believe, and went running through the house, searching. The sick room scent had gone through him, making his teeth chatter even though it had been July.

He remembered the inward faces, the locked expressions. Remembered wondering: *How could this be? Why would she do that?* And the old man's voice droning on in its tired way.

But worst of all—then and now—was that certain, absolute knowledge that she was never coming back. That she was with his father and neither of them was ever coming back.

Why?

What had he done? What had any of them done? Why couldn't she have waited until he was big? Who had made it happen? What would fill the emptiness?

Nothing.

He scuffed the dust with his sound leg, thinking back to the days that had followed. The slow, heavy days that had followed when he had learned the answer. Nothing. So long as he lived there would always be that emptiness.

He sat there on the old buggy seat and his teeth chattered again. He knew old Johnny Reb was going to die, too. Knew it with such certainty that nothing could have shaken his conviction.

Even if the old horse had come walking toward him right then, he still would have known he was going to die. But Johnny Reb didn't come; only shadows came, round and soft and ugly, spreading and thickening as night fell.

Along the roadway saloon lights came on.

The boy got off the buggy seat and started home with the stark memory of pain, of tearing flesh, hot and dry to the knife, the smell of poison spilling out, Jack Swift's big hands, the knife, and the listless eyes of an old horse vivid in his mind.

III

Rob didn't return.

Days flowed. Jack had buried Johnny Reb, knowing it was age more than distemper that had killed him. He'd treated hundreds of horses for distemper and they'd recovered. Johnny Reb had been old—too old, too tired, too willing to leave, so he had gone.

One night a sultry wind blew. A heavy,

bumbling wind that dragged its swollen belly over the barn's roof. Behind it came the sulky growl of thunder. There were massing hosts far overhead in the darkness, rain clouds none could see but knew they were there because the lanterns of the night—the stars—were obscured.

Jack was sprawled in a barrel chair in the harness room. He got up restlessly for no reason at all and walked the length of the barn. The horses were also restless. Static electricity made their manes and tails splay out. Jack went up to the roadway entrance and leaned there with the scent of a storm coming to him. The night was warm, rich with sage fragrance.

The first drops fell just as a hurrying buggy wheeled in with a man and a girl. Jack listened to their pealing laughter. He loosened the check rein loose and led the horse farther back, unharnessed the animal, and stalled it. The man and girl bent into the turmoil of the night, heading across the road. Jack watched them briefly, then backed the rig into place by the shafts. By that time rain was pelting upon the roof, beginning to smack wetly against the hardpan roadway, and glisten along the gutters.

A whooping pair of cowboys went careening past northward, slithering recklessly through the gumbo.

Orange lamplight shone clearly up and down the road and the air was cleaner. Lightning flashed.

The drumming increased and a turbulent burst of thunder shook the town.

Jack stood in the roadside opening of the barn, smelling the cleansed, whirling air. Feeling the storm's wildness. Inwardly responding to the night, to its unshackled swift-running turbulence, its freedom.

For some unrelated and inexplicable reason he thought of the boy, of undersize, thin-faced Rob Logan. Thought that he never should have shown him how distemper is cured by draining. Thinking now, too late, that the fear that lived in Rob was an overwhelming thing, that it blanketed all other emotions under its flooding, moving tide.

Thinking back, step by step, and seeing now that he hadn't been building something between them that pain and fear wouldn't destroy at the first opportunity simply because he'd never really faced Rob's fear. He had failed to make it grow smaller because he hadn't faced it at all; he had simply tried to ignore it. All the while the fear had lain dormant, until an old horse's suffering had brought it up, dark and depthless and encompassing.

The breeze ruffled Jack's hair, heavy and close where his hat had pressed it down, drew out a heavy coil of it, and fled, leaving the curl hanging low upon the man's forehead.

Lightning bolts blasted an eerie, crackling strangeness over the world, too white, too sharp.

And thunder followed with a cannonade close yet distant, echoes running down the glistening darkness. Water thickened in the roadway, chocolate-like, boiling, dissolving manure heaps and prying at the plank walk. It tumbled into crevices to hiss and gush.

Then he saw a blurred figure across the road with a small bag in his hand hunching into the storm, hastening northward. The doctor. Jack's attention fastened upon the form, watching his progress. He could faintly hear the solid clump of footfalls. He last saw the figure, a bobbing, murky outline, shiny-wet, down where the last houses were at the north end of Herd. He thought someone was having a baby, or had slipped in the rain, maybe, and had sprained an ankle or broken an arm. Or perhaps was dying with the gigantic splendor of a summer thunderstorm all around them.

Then he saw another figure, a woman's silhouette this time, coming south along the opposite plank walk toward him. She was covered almost entirely by something coarse, heavy, and rusty-looking—a rain garment of some kind.

He watched her fight through the buffet of the storm, face set indomitably forward as though she was being driven. The way she moved forward with hard intentness, almost ruthlessness, left no doubt that whatever her purpose in being out this night it was urgent.

He was surprised when she stepped down off the walk into the ankle-deep water, heading straight for where he leaned. Then, in a cold flash of lightning, he saw her face—white, wire-tight, cheeks pallid on either side of a full, set mouth, and wide eyes. Without thinking, he moved toward her, held out his hand at the plank walk's edge, and was shocked at the iciness of her grip when she reached forward. He led her into the lee of the barn's overhang. She looked straight into his face.

"Are you Jack?" she asked through rivulets of water.

"Well," he answered wonderingly, "I'm Jack Swift."

"Do you work for Mister Buck?"

"Yes'm."

Uneasiness stirred behind his belt buckle. A premonition. Her cold fingers tightened on his hand. She tugged.

"We've got to hurry."

He let her drag him out into the rain, back through the torrent of the roadway, rain pelting his shoulders like tiny fists. Over the storm he called out: "What is it?"

She looked around, but instead of answering leaned farther into the turbulence breasting each fresh burst of wind and squalling rain with an awesome singleness of purpose, hastening down the night. Several times lightning touched her profile to show the dark brilliance of her eyes and the stubborn thrust of jaw.

She stopped finally before a small, whitewashed house, partly logs, partly planed lumber. Overhead a large sycamore tree groaned and writhed, limbs flinging about in despair, rent by winds with a terrible vengefulness and showering down silver-green leaves. She put her face up close and said: "In there. Go on in. I'll be back in a moment." Her upflung arm pointed rigidly to where a lantern burned low. He looked from the house to her face.

"Who lives there?"

"The Logans." She gave him a push.

He resisted it, turning toward her again. "What's wrong?"

But she was moving away, the rusty, voluminous rain garment gathered close, hurrying up the walk of the house next door.

He stood for only a moment, then a shadow passing in front of the light at the Logan place caught his attention. He went to the door and entered.

A heavily bewhiskered man with a leonine head looked up when Jack's entrance brought with it a raw gust of air. In the sputtering lamplight there was something primeval about him. Small eyes glowed from folds of flesh, heavy arms, and sloping shoulders bulging with strength, and his thick body moved with strange and heavy grace as he delved into a small black bag.

There were also two other men. One was very old; he sniffled constantly. His head was hairless and folded in wrinkles. His eyes, wet and cloudy, seemed only to half grasp events.

The third man continued to gaze at Jack after the others had looked away. He stood unmovingly erect, with a thin, ruddy face carved from stone. His jaw was too heavy for the rest of his features. He said: "Well . . . ?"

When Jack stated his name, the other two men looked up swiftly, studying him. Finally the bear-like man closed his bag and straightened up with a deep sigh. "The lad's in the lean-to," he growled. "And the old man's dead."

"His grandfather?"

"Yes. Died a few minutes ago." The doctor was briefly still, then added: "It's hard on the boy, of course. That's why Amy went for you. He got hysterical and kept repeating your name." The nearly hidden, bright, sardonic eyes lingered on Jack's face. One big-knuckled hand snapped the bag closed with abrupt finality. "I guess she couldn't handle him," the doctor concluded, and started for the door without a backward glance at any of them. When he passed out into the night, the lamps guttered again and the old man peered at one of them and sniffled.

The unmoving man's hard stare was coldly

impersonal. "You're the new hostler at Buck's barn, aren't you?"

"Yes."

As he replied, Jack moved past the icy-eyed man and through the only closed door. The girl was already there, evidently having come there through some rear entrance or hallway. Jack noticed that her rain dress was gone and that she was smaller than he had first thought her to be.

Rob was there, too, cold to the touch and with sweat dappling his thin face. His eyes were expressionless; they looked empty, hollowly sunken in the thinness of his face. Jack moved forward, casting an enormous shadow in the little room. The girl looked up quickly, clearly awed by the way he dwarfed everything else. The only sound was the tumult beyond, in the night.

Jack's hand fell lightly on the boy. At the contact a wild trembling seized Rob. Outside, the wind sucked back suddenly, leaving a stillness. Then the girl's breathing was audible, sharply drawn and cutting. Jack picked the boy up and was surprised at the insignificance of his weight. The trembling lessened. For a moment there was utter silence, then Rob cried. His whole body shook. It was as though a dam had burst except that there was no sound and no tears, just the terrible retching and the scrabbling of small fingers groping along big-muscled arms.

Through the odd burning in the big man's throat

he said: "Easy, boy, easy." This was a totally new experience for him.

Rob's tearing grief went beyond this last, final hurt to a hopelessness that was beyond reasoning, acceptance, or justification. Beyond everything except despair. The big man felt this intuitively. He also felt something else. In other days the boy had said: *Learn to use a gun real good so's folks'd be scairt of you. . . .*

If he had felt that way then, how would he feel a month from now when only the loneliness and bitterness remained?

Jack looked around at the girl. Her full and beautiful mouth was vivid in a locked setting of pallor. There was nothing in her eyes, in her expression, to guide him, so he rocked a little, with rain pounding overhead and occasional growls of thunder thickening the night with a strange power. Finally he spoke, let words flow outward in a soothing way until the trembling died and the wrenching sobs lessened, and his voice filled the room, overriding even the sounds of the storm beyond the solitary window.

His arms ached after a time and his back protested against its hunched-forward position, but he did not move and the entire immensity of the world was squeezed into the lean-to room as his voice droned on.

Then, against his chest, the tumbled hair moved and waxen lips said: "Was it my fault?"

The girl half turned away, eyes hidden behind dark lashes. "Never think that," Jack said.

"Then . . . why?"

Jack looked at the girl again, shared with her the sublimity of knowledge that here, in two words, was something older than man himself, and no one could answer it.

She might have spoken but Jack shook his head. He knew—had lived just that long—what people said now. They mentioned God and His mysterious ways. He also knew that in a small boy's mind hate and fear were lying, waiting to fasten upon something. There must be no mention of God.

He said: "I don't know, Rob. I reckon nobody really knows."

The bowed head moved, gray lips murmured against the big man's chest. He caught only two words: "Johnny Reb. . . ."

He understood and spoke again, with the sounds of the storm atrophying, the intensity of the rain lessening around them, the guttering lamp ceasing to smoke. "Johnny Reb was old, Rob, and he was sick. Inside a horse, like inside a man, is a thing called will. When will dies, so does the horse, or the man. Age takes the will out of things, like it takes the strength away. When an old horse loses his will, he is tired. When he is tired, he wants to lie down and rest."

"But he doesn't want to die!"

The body against Jack's chest stiffened in protest.

"Sure, son," the big man said softly. "Death isn't hurt. It isn't pain or fear. It's rest."

"My grandpaw wouldn't want to go away from me."

Jack could feel the heartbeats. "Your grandpaw needed rest," he said. "You'd want him to have that, wouldn't you?"

"My mother wasn't old . . . she wasn't tired."

"Son, sickness is like age. It takes away the will, too. It makes folks want to rest."

Jack looked at the girl. Her back was fully to him now. He looked past her at the drab wall, crooked where the log foundation had settled. Rob relaxed a little in his arms and Jack knew that because he and the boy had shared sorrow together, twice now, they would never be apart again, for in them both dwelt a might of loneliness, each had to gather up the pieces of their lives and start over again.

Then Rob slept, slumped imperceptibly against the big man with his breathing deep and soft, broken only by an occasional drawn-out shudder.

Jack put him to bed. The girl helped. They turned his face toward the wall and away from the light. When they both straightened up beside the cot, the girl said: "I can't cry any more."

Jack ignored that. "What happened with his grandfather?"

"He had a stroke. He was very old. Since his daughter died . . . well . . . like you said, the will to live was gone."

Watching the shadowed, thin face, Jack said: "What becomes of him now?"

The girl returned to her chair. "I suppose Josh will take him."

"Josh?"

"Josh Logan . . . his father's brother. Rob's uncle."

Jack remembered the heavy-jawed man. "Was he in the other room with the doctor and that old man?"

"Yes. The old man was a crony of Rob's grandfather. They were buffalo hunters many years ago. The people around Herd call him Uncle Ned."

Jack was thinking of Josh Logan's cold and hostile look. "This uncle," he said slowly. "Are you sure he'll want the boy?"

The girl was long enough in answering for Jack to know her thoughts. "Josh is Rob's only living relative . . . but I don't know. Rob's father and Josh Logan hadn't spoken in years before Rob's father was killed. And . . . Josh despised Rob's mother."

Jack made a cigarette, sucked life into it from the lamp, and studied the girl's face. The house was as still as the night. The storm had passed, finally, and only the drip of water beyond the window and an infrequent soughing of wind through the sycamore tree outside remained.

The girl squared herself in the chair. "What did he mean about Johnny Reb?" she asked.

"An old horse by that name that belonged to Buck. He died of distemper a few weeks ago."

"Oh."

Lamplight limned the rounded fullness of her figure and it also deepened the dark shadows under her eyes. The world dissolved from the room until only she was left in the big man's gaze, solemn and still.

"Are you a relative?" he inquired.

She shook her head. "No, I live next door." The dark lashes swept up to reveal an intense gaze. "Would you take him?"

It caught him totally unprepared. He stared at her as though he wasn't sure he had heard right. Then he looked down at the cigarette in his hand.

"I'm no kin, ma'am. Besides, I haven't anything to offer a kid."

She arose, still watching him, then she looked away, toward the thin sleeping figure on the cot. "No, of course not," she said. There was a long interval of silence before she swung to face him. "He didn't ask for his uncle when the doctor told him his grandfather had died . . . he asked for you."

Jack crushed out the cigarette, turned, and looked out the window. "He's not an orphan, ma'am."

"I don't believe Josh Logan will care."

He faced around. "No, why not?"

"For one thing he's a bachelor. For another, he's superintendent of the railroad company's right of way department and track crews. He's not home very much." She looked down at the cot again. "I just can't picture him making a home for a little boy."

There was another interval of silence. Then the girl spoke again.

"I suppose I'll have to make funeral arrangements."

Jack said: "You? Why not Logan . . . at least he's kin."

"I doubt that he'll do it."

Jack's gaze clouded. He moved closer to the girl. "Maybe you'd better tell me the whole story," he said.

She answered him without looking away from the cot. "It's an old story around Herd. Josh Logan wanted to marry Rob's mother. She married his brother instead. Josh is not a forgiving man. That's all I know, really. There's a lot of gossip of course, but those are the facts."

Recalling Josh Logan's face, Jack said: "They're probably enough."

She put a hand on his arm. "Why don't you take him? You could give him so much more than Josh could."

He looked into her eyes, wondering if there

would be any point in saying that vengeful men, like lost little boys, had hatred living in them that needed only an image to fasten upon to become deadly? He decided from the look of her face she would not understand, and moved away from her touch. Then, to gain time for thought, he said: "Did you know Rob's mother?"

A dark shadow crossed her face when she answered. "Yes. I knew his father, too, but I wasn't much older than Rob when he was killed. I knew them all. I knew his grandfather was dying."

"How did you know that?"

"He told me. I don't see how he held on as long as he did. He was very old and he was ill." Her gaze grew introspective. "I don't see how they faced the things that happened to them. There wasn't anything but suffering . . . for years." She shook off the mood and raised her eyes. "If Josh Logan has no objection to you raising Rob, you could live here. It belongs to Rob now."

Jack went to the chair and dropped down. He stared at the meager figure under the quilts on the cot. "I don't know anything about kids," he said. "I've always been a drifter. . . ."

"I can tell you this . . . you will both be good for each other."

He got up, thoughts weaving in and out of his mind, distorted by the emotional draining he had experienced. "I've got to think about this," he said, and went to the door. "You'll take care of him tonight, ma'am?"

"Yes."

He cast a final look at the sleeping boy, nodded to the girl, and left them.

IV

Josh Logan was standing behind his desk. When Jack passed through the office doorway and saw him there, he thought Logan was as withdrawn and distant as the moon.

Jack closed the door and waited. Logan made no motion toward a chair, offered no hand, or indicated in any way that his visitor was welcome.

Jack moved through the coldness in the room. "You may remember me," he said. "I was at Logan's the night the old man died."

"I remember," Logan said, coldly impersonal eyes like agate. "What do you want?"

"I came to talk about the boy . . . Rob."

"Yes."

Logan didn't make it easy. Jack had trouble making the words come out right.

"Well, I've been told you travel a lot and maybe you wouldn't want to be bothered with a kid. I could take him, teach him a little, sort of help him along. We get along fine."

"At Buck's barn?" Logan's lips scarcely parted.

"He never should have been allowed down there in the first place."

Jack reacted to Logan's obvious antagonism. They were of a height and now their eyes met in silent struggle.

"There are worse places than livery barns, Mister Logan," the big man said. "And he could learn the saddler's trade there . . . and other things, too."

"You'd teach him, Swift?" The cold eyes flicked up and down and back to Jack's face. "What else would you teach him?"

"What d'you mean?"

"I mean you don't wear a gun."

"What of it?"

Logan moved up, sat down behind the desk, and raised his eyes. "It's against the law for ex-felons to wear guns. In my work with railroad track gangs I meet a lot of men, Swift. I can spot an ex-convict a mile off. That's what I mean."

Jack was silent. Logan touched some papers on his desk, then leaned back. "If the boy's to learn something, better teachers can be found," he said. "For example, he could study telegraphy under one of my men."

"Even if he'd much rather work around horses and saddles?"

"What would a boy like that know about what's good for him? He's immature." Logan's eyes glowed. "So were his parents."

Jack struggled to hold his temper, and lost. He leaned forward from the hips when next he spoke. "Immature?" he said. "I can think of something that's a lot worse than immaturity . . . hating a kid's parents even after they're dead and keeping that hatred alive against the kid . . . that's worse than immaturity, Logan."

Logan sprang up and for a moment Jack thought he would attack him. His face went white and his hands clenched into fists. When he spoke, his voice was sharp-honed and harsh.

"Swift, I'm going to give you some advice. You've gone out of your way to meddle in my affairs. I won't forget that. You'd better learn your place. It wouldn't be hard to send you back where you came from . . . Yuma. Now get out of here."

Seeing the white and deadly heat of Logan's anger, Jack knew his chances of ever moving Logan were forever ruined. He left the office and walked aimlessly through the hot afternoon. Walked without heeding direction and ultimately found himself farther south than he had intended to go. Across the road was the sheriff's office, a small, plain building, sturdily doored and barred at the windows. The sight raised ghosts in his mind. He turned back, went as far as the barn, and saw Buck watching him from the doorway.

When he turned in, the old man jerked his head backward in a conspiratorial manner and gestured toward the harness room. Jack frowned. Buck then puckered up his face and hissed: "Amy Southard's back there, waiting for you."

Jack went to the harness room doorway and stopped, filling the opening. The girl's soft, anxious eyes leaped to his face.

"What did he say?"

"He said no." Jack moved into the room and leaned against a harness rack. "He also said some other things, too. I gathered he's figuring on putting Rob with a telegrapher . . . or someone like that."

"With whom?"

"He didn't say."

Amy sat down in the barrel chair and looked at her hands. As though from a distance she said: "Rob's at our house. When I left, my mother was getting his breakfast."

"That's fine," the big man said hollowly, not looking at her.

"Jack, what will you do now?"

"Do?" he said, looking at her with exasperation. "Nothing. What can I do?"

She arose, looked him straight in the face, then started for the door. As she brushed past, he caught her arm.

"Wait."

She stopped. Her beauty was clear even in the dingy atmosphere of the harness room. He let go of her arm.

"I did some thinking while I was walking back

here. Maybe it'd be better if Rob did learn a trade like that. Telegraphers sit down. And another thing. . . ."

"Didn't you tell Rob there would always be a demand for good saddle makers? Isn't that largely a sitting-down job, too? But even if it wasn't . . . should he surrender to his limp . . . plan his life so he's defeated before he even starts to live? A lot of people limp, Jack. We've had presidents who limped. Andrew Jackson did."

He didn't look at her, but her eyes never left his face. Then she went on speaking. "There are some other things you've forgotten, too. He wants to be a saddle maker. But the most tragic thing is that there's something he needs even more than a trade . . . love. Every time he's loved something it's been taken away from him."

"I know all those things," he said.

She took another step through the doorway before saying: "Yes, I suppose you do. You just don't want to do anything about them."

"That's not true," he answered quickly. "I just don't know what to do."

"I'll tell you, Jack . . . fight. Fight for his happiness."

He looked at her. Fight Logan, the man who knew why he didn't wear a gun? It wasn't that simple. "Listen, Miss Southard," he said tightly, "Logan's legal kin . . . I'm just a drifter."

"You are the only person left on this earth that

Rob loves. You're the only person he doesn't believe will let him down."

"That's putting it pretty strongly," he said.

"No, Jack, that's stating the simple truth. If you went into court for the boy and he was asked to make a choice between you and Logan, he'd pick you without a moment's hesitation."

The big man's eyes widened. "No," he said in a sudden, sharp tone. "It can't come to that."

"Why not?"

"It just can't, that's all."

As she stared at him, her eyes widened, her lips parted slightly, and for a moment they were close, looking into each other's eyes. Then she turned away from the doorway and passed from his sight.

Moments later old Buck came up. He took a squinted long look at Jack's face and let the words lying upon his lips die. Instead, he said: "I expect we'd better grease axles today."

Jack greased axles that day. The following day he hauled meadow hay in a wagon. The third day he worked on the seal-brown mare's contracted hoof with sweat pouring off him and heel flies exploring his ears when both his hands were occupied. He spoke little and could not shake off the self-reproach that failed to atrophy as the days passed.

Time ran on, the days of late summer flowed one after another, like gold, and gradually the ranchers, freighters, and even the townsmen came to bring their saddles and harness to Buck's barn for repairing, even though Herd had a saddler, old Charley Schmidt. This work kept Jack occupied far into the night nearly every day. It also made Buck grow pensive. Finally he went to Jack with an idea.

"Folks are getting to know you better as a saddler than as a liveryman," he said. "Now I got this notion. Charley Schmidt's old and I've heard a rumor that he wants to quit business. You could buy him out some way and set yourself up as a saddle maker. Take over Charley's shop. How's it sound to you?"

"Sounds fine, Buck, only I don't have that kind of money."

"Pshaw, I'll loan it to you."

They went to see Schmidt. The old man was glad to sell. He was even gladder to spend several weeks at the shop until Jack was established. They complemented one another; Charley was talkative and Jack Swift rarely spoke at all.

Summer finally came to its prolonged, dusty close and Jack *belonged* as he had never imagined that he could. He had customers, friends, acceptance and respect, even though he wore no gun in a land where a gun on the hip was as common as the trousers under it. But in the secret place of his mind he never forgot Amy Southard or crippled Rob Logan.

He didn't see either of them. Hadn't seen them

in fact in many weeks. Twice he had thought he'd glimpsed Amy but he wasn't sure.

He worked in the shop and prospered, and, when the sheriff came by to visit one day, only a little of the old uneasiness returned.

He made living quarters behind the shop in a lean-to. They were tight for a man of his size but they were comfortable and private. There was only one drawback to them—at night they were peopled with faces from the past.

He walked for exercise. He neither owned a horse nor had any use for one. He walked nearly every night and came to know every byway, every footpath, and most of the little meandering roadways for several miles around Herd. He also followed the creek by moonlight, listening to the splash of trout, and knew where the best fishing holes were without fishing any of them.

He grew into the warp of Herd without becoming a part of its social life. He was a reserved person, a big and powerful man whose integrity was beyond the expectation of those who brought him work, but a loner, a person who preferred his own company to the company of others—or so it seemed to the people who came to know him.

Then, one late afternoon in early fall, he looked up from the cutting table as a thin shadow hovered in the doorway, and a sequence of events began that Herd would remember for many years.

"Hello, Jack."

The small face was thinner and the limp seemed more pronounced. The boy appeared old and wizened. The change held Jack motionless for a second, before he smiled.

"Howdy, Rob. Haven't seen you in a 'coon's age."

The boy's blue eyes ranged over the shop. Over racks of leather and hanging saddles, rows of bridles, reins, bits, chaps, harness, a world of rich fragrance and craftsmanship.

The boy said: "Gosh, you sure have a swell shop."

Jack wiped his hands on the apron he wore and reached for his tobacco sack. "Come on in," he said, and heard the soft drag of foot leather across the floor.

"This is swell, Jack. Do you make new saddles, too?"

"On order, Rob. Now and then. Right now there's a big rush for harness." Jack lit up and exhaled. "The cowmen're getting ready for roundup." He looked into the wistful blue eyes. "How've you been, anyway. Learning to be a telegrapher?"

"Telegrapher?" the boy said, touching a new saddle reverently. "No, I guess I didn't have the touch for that. Anyway Mister Cavin said I didn't."

"Who's he, the telegrapher?"

"No, he's the man I live with."

"Oh. Well, what are you learning?"

"Nothing much, I guess. How to milk goats, cook a little, maybe."

The blue eyes lifted to his face and the man saw something hard there. Hard and secretive.

"Do you ever see Amelia?"

"Who?"

"Amy Southard. That girl who lived next door to my grandfather's place. Do you ever see her?"

"No. Do you?"

Rob shook his head. "No. I'm not supposed to."

"Why not?"

"I don't know exactly. My uncle told Mister Cavin not to let me see her . . . or you, either."

The cigarette was dead between the big man's fingers. He put it aside and said: "Oh."

"I sneaked down here today, though."

The man's eyes followed the boy's hand as it went out to rest lightly on a new pair of shotgun chaps lying across a saddle. The boy's voice came softly.

"Jack. Maybe if you asked Mister Cavin if I could come down here, he'd let me."

Through the ensuing silence traffic sounds from the roadway came in past the door with distinct clarity. Dogs barked, men called to one another, and horses at the tie racks blew their noses. People stumped past on the plank walk and a little autumnal zephyr groped along under the eaves making a sad sound.

"Jack . . . I got a gun."

The man's gray eyes, cloudy with indecision, grew still. "What kind of a gun?"

"A Colt six-shooter. It's sort of rusty but it shoots."

"How do you know it shoots?"

The blue eyes wavered. "Well, Mister Cavin keeps bullets in a tin can. I took some and tried it." The boy half turned away. "But I'm not very good with it yet."

"Yet? Lord, all it takes to be good with a gun is the will. Shoot and shoot and shoot until you never miss, then draw and draw and draw until you're a blur of speed." Jack's hands felt damp. He wiped them on the apron again and straightened up. "Rob, we've been pardners sort of for a long time, haven't we?"

"Yes."

"And if your pardner asked you to do him a favor . . . you'd do it, wouldn't you?"

"Yes."

"Then bring me that gun."

The boy only hesitated a second before he said: "I will. The next time I can slip away. Jack . . . would you ask Mister Cavin for me . . . about coming down here once in a while? I wouldn't be in the way here because I wasn't in the way at Buck's barn."

"You wouldn't be in the way, son."

"He might not give in right away. He's sort of bull-headed sometimes."

"Is he? What's he do for a living, Rob?"

"Works for my uncle on one of the track gangs. That's how I sneaked away today. He had to go out to where they're having trouble with some new track."

"Have you seen your uncle lately?"

"No, he doesn't come around. Just that once . . . when he came for me at Amy's house." The blue eyes brightened. "Boy, Amy sure gave him a tongue-lashing that day."

"What about?"

The boy's expression clouded over, became detached and distant. "I don't remember much of it. I guess it was about him not letting me live at the barn with you."

"Well, that wouldn't have been a very good place to live."

"This would be, though."

Jack untied the apron strings slowly, removed the covering, and tossed it on the cutting table. "Will Mister Cavin come home and find you gone?" he asked.

Rob's glance came to rest on Jack's face. "I guess I'd better go," he said.

"You won't forget to bring me the gun?"

"No, I won't forget."

The boy left, his crippled, slow gait heightened by reluctance. For a long time afterward Jack leaned against the cutting table without moving. Stood there woodenly with thoughts spiraling upward in his mind. And later, when he lit the lamps and went back to work, lines drawn around patterns on the sides of leather blurred. He finally went to a chair and dropped down.

His own youth returned with hurting vividness. He saw a lanky, hot-eyed rebel with his first gun. He hadn't found it any more than Rob had found his gun . . . he'd stolen it. He'd gotten cartridges the same way. Then there had been days of practicing, of stubborn, blind perseverance. Of eventual unerring accuracy. Then more days of drawing, of turning holsters flesh side out, smooth side inward. Drawing, working the gun around until it rode loose. Of waxing the inside of the holster. Drawing and firing until reflexes were automatic, blurred by speed, like lightning. Weeks and months of co-ordinating the two accomplishments. Deadly accuracy and blinding speed. Days and weeks and months of practice. Then. . . .

He got up swiftly and crossed to the cutting table. Folded his arms across his chest and leaned there, remembering. The first fight had been with a drunken, loud-mouthed cowboy. It had been so easy. The cowboy's gun wasn't even clear of its holster when the third eye appeared in his forehead.

Then—two years of hell-roaring wildness. Fights, drunks, robberies, killings by one of the fastest guns in the territory—and finally an ambush with a herd of stolen horses, a gunfight, captivity, the trial, and three years in the Yuma prison.

Now, at thirty-one and on the road back, he faced an image of himself. Not so big and raw perhaps but with more reason to practice with a gun. With Rob there was that haunting deformity and a sense of deep resentment—with him there'd been only wildness. Rob was walking the same trail. The same road to Yuma—if he was lucky— to a shallow grave in some unknown boothill cemetery if he was unlucky.

He thought of the clear blue eyes, the long, thin fingers, and dread moved deep in him. Enough practice would make Rob Logan a gunman second to none. It was in the boy to be that good, and who would know it better than Jack Swift of old Tularosa?

It was in him to be the best at anything he undertook. He was sensitive, observant, perfectly co-ordinated in all ways except for that crooked leg—and that was going to be the cause of his own eventual destruction, the way he was going now, and worse even, the destruction of dozens of others as well. That leg, a sense of being wronged—and an old gun.

Jack swooped up his hat, clamped it on, and left the shop. Evening shadows were coming. He walked through the cooling night as far as Buck's barn and stopped where the short liveryman was straining to reach up far enough to light the coach lamps.

"Damned hired help," the old man grumbled. "Forgets to light these cussed things every damned night." He got the last wick burning, dropped down flat-footed, and squinted upward. "I never wanted to be as tall as you are . . . except when I have to light those blasted things."

Buck shook his head at the lamps, then jerked his head sideways. "Come on, I got some harness needs mending," he said.

But Jack stood still. "Do you know a man named Cavin, Buck?"

"Cavin? Cavin. Yes, I expect I do. Would he be Ernie Cavin who works for the railroad?"

"Yes. Where does he live?"

"Well," the old man said, looking northward. "You know where my house is?"

"Yes."

"And the next place is an old log house?"

"Yes."

"Two houses beyond that, north, is a little shack that sets back a piece inside an old stake fence. That's Cavin's place." Buck's rheumy glance sharpened. "He owe you money?"

"No."

"Then you must be the only man in Herd he don't owe. Still, he's not a bad feller when he's sober."

"Is he a drunk?"

The rheumy eyes twinkled. "I wouldn't go that far. But Ernie gets his share . . . and danged if I don't believe he sometimes gets my share, too."

"Thanks."

Jack crossed the road with the wind flattening his shirt and whipping up little gobbets of dust around his boots. He stepped up onto the far plank walk and started along it. The pleasant odor of white-oak smoke was in the air. He scarcely noticed it.

He had to pass the Southard place and the half-log, half-plank house where Rob's grandfather had died, to get where he was going. The Logan place was forlornly dark but the Southard house was cheerily alight. He didn't see the pale shadow on the porch in the darkening night as he swung past. It stirred quickly as he passed as though in recognition.

Passing through Ernie Cavin's gate wasn't a matter of opening it; he stepped over it where it lay in the grass. A broken whiskey bottle lay near. He saw it about the time the goat smell struck him. By that time he was moving toward the front door, which hung ajar.

Beyond the opening, highlighted by a lamp with a dirty mantle, was a man sprawled in a broken chair. Farther back a thin face was locked in concentration at a cook stove. A box in a corner of the room contained a sick goat kid. There was an overpowering stench to the room, and, as the man standing in darkness looked in, he saw all the squalor and filth with one sweeping glance. His fist, raised in mid-air to knock, hung motionless. The sprawled man coughed and spat.

Jack's fist fell back to his side. He turned, went down past the broken gate, and out onto the plank walk. For a moment he breathed deeply, then he started southward back toward the shop. He did not see the opalescent apparition materialize at the Southards' gate until a voice halted him.

"Mister Swift?"

He turned and saw her face. "Yes?"

"Is something wrong?"

He stared at her hard. "Why, no, ma'am, nothing's wrong. Just a kid and a drunk and a shack full of goats."

"It's taken you a long time to find it out."

The savage look he gave her made her draw up erect. Then he turned abruptly away and continued on his way.

The months of indecision and reluctance crystallized in him. He stumped past men who nodded and didn't see them, past shafts of lamplight that shone upon the fierce anger that was raging within him. He forgot the night and the people in it until a small, gnomish silhouette barred his path.

"Whoa, boy," old Buck said. "You look like a stampede goin' somewhere to happen."

Jack ground to a wide-legged halt, big and glaringly silent.

"I know," the liveryman said. "I know how it is. I've known all along. So have other folks. Figured one day you'd find out . . . and meanwhile I've been doin' a heap of thinking. Now listen to me for a minute. . . ." Buck touched his sleeve. "You're not listenin'."

"To what? What is there to say? You don't put a kid out like that any more than you'd let a man have a horse when you knew he used a loaded quirt."

"But you got to use some sense."

"Yeah?"

"Sure."

"How come you to know about it, Buck, and not me?"

"Amy. She comes around to visit once in a while. She's asked a heap of questions about you, too. 'Course, I couldn't answer 'em and ain't certain I would have, if I'd known the answers."

"Never mind the girl. Have you seen . . . ?"

"Boy, you got to be careful. Don't go off half-cocked. Josh Logan's no upstart. A lot of men work for him. You got to sit down and think things over before you do anything. Logan's a bad man to cross. Real bad, Jack."

"Am I supposed to stand by and watch him take his crazy hatred for dead people out on a little kid?"

"He won't hurt the boy."

"You mean he won't use a loaded quirt. How about making him live with a drunk, keeping him penned up with goats, cooking goat stew for a drunk in a place that smells like an outhouse?"

Buck stood, warp-legged, listening, wisely saying nothing and letting the big man's fury run its course. He was old and understanding.

"I knew what you were about when you come to the barn a while back asking about Cavin," he said, finally, when Jack became silent. "That's why I walked over here. To head you off. But listen, Jack; hard knocks make a kid just like they make a man."

Swift's retort was bitter. "Who knows that better'n me? But not like that, Buck. Not living like that? In a place that stinks worse than the garbage dump."

"I didn't have it much different when I grew up, Jack. Lots of us didn't."

"Yeah, and look what lots of us turned out to be, too. Besides, does that make it necessary for him? Hard knocks on a full belly are one thing, especially if you're learning something . . . growing up maybe. Like being kicked for walking too close behind a strange horse. You learn that way. This way . . . all he's learning is how deep filth is. And, Buck . . . that kid's got hatred growing in him. I know. I saw it. And he's got something else, too, but you'd never believe it because he's just a kid. I know about that, too. I know what it can lead to."

Jack raised a thick arm and let it fall. Buck leaned upon a building and kept his voice low when he spoke.

"All right, Jack, but you raising hell is going to hurt the kid, not help him. You raise a hand against Logan an' both you 'n' the kid'll think the sky fell on you. You got to do some calm thinking."

Jack felt in a shirt pocket for his tobacco sack. His head dropped and his fingers worked like the claws of a spider while Buck went on speaking.

"Do what you can for the boy, but do it on the sly. Help him whenever you can . . . but don't let Logan find out you're doin' it . . . and for gosh sakes don't tangle with Logan. There's talk he don't cotton to you anyway."

Buck studied the big man's face, saw that the anger was ashes now, pushed off the wall, and touched Swift's arm lightly.

"Go on home now and cool down," he concluded. "You'll think different in the morning. Good night."

Jack took Buck's advice. He went to the shop, locked the front door behind him, and passed through to his lean-to living quarters.

More time passed, days of cooling sunlight and crystal-clear nights. Then one day two weeks later Amy Southard came into the shop with a hurrying step. He saw the anxiety on her face and arose from the sewing horse, crossed to the counter, and spread his hands on it, palms downward.

"Where is he, Mister Swift?"

"Where is who?"

"Rob."

He knew, as surely as he knew anything, what she was talking about, but so far he had not heard anything.

"Tell me about it," he said quietly.

"He's run away."

The big man removed his apron, balled it up, and tossed it onto the cutting table. "You know more than that," he said.

She pushed the words at him. "Ernie Cavin went out on the line yesterday morning, and, when he returned last night, Rob wasn't there. He waited until this morning to say anything."

"Yeah. Passed out waited."

"He reported it to Sheriff Hoyt Farmer." She was holding his gaze with her eyes. "I was sure he'd come to you."

"He didn't."

"But surely you have an idea where he went."

"I couldn't even guess. I have no idea at all."

"Oh," the girl said. "Why didn't he come to one of us?"

"I reckon you know why," Jack said heavily.

Amy nodded, watching him, then she turned slowly, went to the doorway, and passed from sight beyond.

Jack waited until her footfalls died away, then put on his coat, picked up his hat, and left the shop. He went south along the plank walk as far as the sheriff's office. Sheriff Farmer was standing by his saddle horse at the hitch rail outside the jailhouse, watching him approach. He nodded gravely.

" 'Evening, Mister Swift."

" 'Evening, Sheriff. About that kid that disappeared. . . ."

"Yeah. Little Rob Logan, the crippled kid. What about him?"

"Well, I was wondering if you needed any help looking for him. I sort of liked him."

"I know," the lawman said, looking up the roadway with his solemn glance. "I don't imagine there's much need for you to ride out, though. His uncle's got a posse of railroaders searching for him. I expect they'll find him all right."

The unwavering glance swung back to Jack's face. "I'd go myself except that someone stole a Morgan stud horse from Perc Merton's place last night." The sheriff shortened the reins in his hands and popped them together. "Bad business, horse stealin'."

"Yeah."

Sheriff Farmer straightened up off the hitch rack. "Anyway, kids all run off one time or another . . . even as you and I did. I don't expect this'll come to much."

Jack left the lawman standing by his horse. He did not know that Hoyt Farmer was watching him walk away with a look of interest on his face. He didn't know, and, if he had known, he wouldn't have cared.

V

Jack walked back toward the shop as far as the first saloon. There, he sank down upon a bench.

He remembered the Merton place. It was about a mile from town. About as far as a kid with a crooked leg could walk. First the gun, then the bullets, now the stolen horse.

It would have taken every last shred of Rob's courage to approach the stud horse, saddle and bridle him, get into the saddle, and ride off in the darkness. So—the kid was desperate beyond despair. He was fighting the biggest battle of his life. Not only against goat smell and a vomiting drunkard, but against his own fear, against his own bitter, fear-filled world. He was rebelling with everything that was in him against everything he knew—pain, fear, bewilderment, and ridicule—and he was doing it now on a stolen horse, with a gun he knew passably well how to handle, a handful of bullets—and with a determination only he and Jack Swift could fathom.

Rob would follow a pattern. Unless he was

stopped, he would become something Sheriff Farmer, Amy Southard, or even Josh Logan would not understand.

Jack knew. It took a man who had also started life on the sundown trail to understand this, to realize how the boy would be waiting out there somewhere, high on a windy ridge, watching his back trail, full of rebellion, desperation, and hate.

An unexpected shadow loomed up. It was Sheriff Farmer's left-handed deputy, Will Spencer, a lean, capable man with whom Jack had often been friendly. Spencer was known for the briefness of his speech and the swiftness of his draw.

He said: "Good evenin', Jack."

"Hello, Will."

"You seen Amy Southard tonight?"

"I saw her about sundown."

Spencer leaned on an upright and studied the big man's face. "She's plumb upset."

"I know."

"The boy'll turn up."

"Yeah," Jack replied dryly. "He'll turn up . . . about five years from now . . . with a fast horse, two guns, and a chip on his shoulder."

Will Spencer's hooded eyes widened perceptibly. "A fast horse . . . ?"

Jack got up and faced around. Seeing the slow look of understanding, he said: "Will, how far would you go on a crooked leg? Just about that far, wouldn't you?"

Spencer was thoughtfully silent for a time, then he began to wag his head in disbelief. "Naw, I don't believe it. Why, Rob'd be scairt stiff of a stud horse."

"Is he a mean horse, Will?"

"No, he's well-mannered, but you know how they snort and paw and roll their eyes." Another wag of the head and Spencer said: "Naw, the kid wouldn't have the grit for that, Jack."

Jack turned away. You couldn't make people understand. They'd never believe what desperation could make a kid do—unless they'd been driven that far themselves. He went to Buck's barn, hired a big chestnut horse from the night hawk, and was swinging aboard when someone spoke his name from the shadows. It was Deputy Spencer again; he was coming down the alleyway.

"Swift? Glad I caught you before you left. Josh Logan wants to see you. He was by your shop but it was closed."

Jack shortened the reins. "What about? I'm in a hurry."

"Well," the deputy drawled, "he seems to think you encouraged the kid to run away."

"He's a damned liar!"

Spencer shrugged. "Tell him that, not me," he said. "You goin' to see him?"

"Maybe when I get back. Not now."

"You goin' to look for the kid?"

"Yes."

"It's a pretty big country."

"I know that."

"Any idea where you're going to look?"

Jack edged the horse up toward the roadside doorway. "None at all." He nodded at Buck, who had come up, and rode out. For a time the liveryman and deputy watched his progress through town. Buck looked secretly pleased about something.

"Big feller, ain't he?" he said to the lawman.

Spencer nodded, still watching Jack ride out. "Yeah, he's big."

"Be a hard man to whip if he was mad."

"Yeah."

"If I was Logan, I wouldn't go out of my way to start a fight with him."

Will Spencer looked around. "Logan's no greener, either, Buck. That boot'd fit both feet."

"Logan," Buck said flatly, "has lots of hired help but damned few friends. I got a notion in a mix-up like this friends'd count."

Will Spencer continued to regard the old man for a while in silence, then he left. Walked as far as the roadway and looked north. Jack Swift was growing small out along the stage road. He was riding toward the fork in the road where a scraggly old juniper tree stood. Nailed to its trunk was a roughly lettered sign with names on it and an arrow pointing westerly. WILL CALDWELL   C.B. SWINNERTON PAUL VISHER DIAMOND O RANCH P. MERTON.

He took the left fork and followed wagon ruts lying like twin snakes where they threw themselves up and over a barren ridge, then down a steady slope to a juncture with another road. There, a second sign pointed the way to the Merton place, and later, as Jack was riding into a yard where gusts of autumn wind made loose gates squeak, a big man, old and gaunt, came out to watch him approach. He rode up and swung down.

"Howdy."

"Howdy."

"Is this where the stud horse was stolen from?"

"It is. You a new deputy?"

"No," Jack answered. "Mind showing me where he was taken from?"

"Don't mind at all," the old man said. "Come on."

They walked beyond the edge of the stony yard. There, the old man raised an arm. "Yonder. See that 'ere pole corral? That's it. I kept him down there so's he wouldn't be a-squealin' every time someone rode a mare into the yard."

Jack looked beyond the corral toward the blue-tiered, long lift of mountains. In the near distance some horses were grazing. "Those your animals, too?" he asked.

"Yep. Got about eighty head. Whoever stoled my stud horse knew better'n try to catch one of them."

Jack studied the corral. A crippled kid would know he couldn't catch loose horses. The old man's voice was running on.

"I got a notion that 'ere horse thief knowed my stud."

"Looks that way," Jack said, drawing the livery horse up close, toeing in, and swinging up. "Did you look for sign?"

"Yep." A thin arm shot up, pointing westward. "I tracked him out a piece . . . 'most as far as the lava beds . . . about six miles from here. Then come back and went to town to tell Sheriff Farmer. Catchin' horse thieves is his job, not mine. Besides, I got chores to do." The old man's arm dropped. He studied Jack a moment, then frowned. "If you figure to track that feller, you'd best get damned well ahead of them railroaders. They're tramplin' the sign right out of sight."

"How many railroaders?"

"Seven. Josh Logan sent 'em out this mornin' all mounted on big team horses. Damnedest sight you ever seen. I showed 'em the tracks and away they went a-whoopin' and a-hollerin' like a band of Apaches." Merton spat. "Hell, they'll get no farther than the lava beds. Some of 'em could hardly speak English. As trackers they couldn't find their backsides with both hands an' a candle."

Jack nodded and reined around. "Thanks."

The old man took a few steps beside the horse. "Figure you can find the thief?" he asked.

"I can sure try," Jack replied.

He rode directly to the pole corral and picked up the broad trail of Logan's men. It was wide and clear. He kicked the chestnut into a long lope and rode steadily until evening grayness swept in, fast. Then he sighted the railroaders up ahead a short mile. They were milling around, apparently confused by something. When he got closer, Jack saw what it was. Old Man Merton's lava bed turned out to be obsidian, as slick as glass, as shiny, and just as treacherous to a mounted man on a shod horse.

Without a second thought Jack swung wide in a northerly way and by-passed the railroaders. Once a call sounded and he looked around. A man waved. He ignored it and kept on going.

Irony was in his expression. A scared kid using obsidian to hide his trail was a long way from panicking. Rob had won the first round; his uncle's men were stymied at the glass rock.

He rode until evening came with great, florid splashes of red upon the gray horizon, strokes a thousand miles long reflecting downward from the tucked-up gut of heaven. He left the wide plain of obsidian behind, buttoned his coat against the chill of dusk, and off-saddled when it became too dark to see tracks any longer. Wind whimpered through the grass above a lee gully nearby. He hobbled the chestnut and lay down with the saddle blanket over him.

When he found Rob—what? Take him back to Cavin's goat shed? Hand him over to Logan's crushing hatred? He pressed flatter against the ground and tucked his collar in, against the cold fingers of a fall night.

Or just take the gun away from him, give him some money, and tell him to keep on going? That would be easiest. No, Logan wouldn't accept that and, anyway, the boy would be exactly where he was right now—hating, rebelling, and running. Then—what?

Night came fully after a while. The sky was clean-swept by a high wind. There was a hint of rain-like electricity in the air. Coyotes tongued in the distance and the livery horse worked his ears uneasily over their sound. Somewhere in the blue blackness a cow bawled, got a quavering answer, and became silent. Night owls skimmed past on silent wings, low, and the grass stirred uneasily where mice, catching some instinctive warning, raced for cover.

Overhead the stars looked down impersonally. Jack stirred. It was easy to say—"I don't know."—but it solved nothing. And there was a heap at stake, too. More than a stolen stud horse, more than Amy's anxiety, Logan's anger, or the sheriff's mild interest. There was a future at stake, a boy's belief that the world was a dry shuck of a place. Saying—"I don't know."—didn't help a bit. Of course, he didn't know what to do—what man would have known? But all the same he had to do something.

He fell asleep on that, but before the first streaks of dawn appeared off in the east, he was heading northwest again, walking ahead of the saddled horse, taking plenty of time to read the prints on the shadowed ground.

The new day brightened gradually, took on the color of diluted blood. There was a somber silence to it; the rain-like electricity was stronger than ever.

When it was light enough to make out tracks from the saddle, Jack mounted up and pushed on. Finally he hauled up, studying the land ahead. He could go on a yard at a time until Doomsday and never catch up. He'd always get up where Rob had been, but that way he'd never get where he was.

The sprawl of land was lavish. Westerly the country was more or less open with scattered patches of sage and chaparral, a few squatty trees, mostly junipers, an occasional piñon or the burst glory of late-blooming paloverdes, green trunks slim and graceful. But it was too open a country for a boy to use who had had sense enough to cross obsidian to hide his tracks.

Northward was forest, rising up mountain slopes to a purple, hazy crest. It was a wild, hushed world of its own. Easterly lay foothills, more trees and more open spaces. Jack rode in that direction, kept to it until he crossed an old roadbed and found the stud horse's unshod hoof marks turning along it, following it toward those far-away hills.

Jack reined up again, farther along, wondering why Rob was following the road instead of heading directly into the hills. Up to now his diversion tactics had been excellent. Then he saw the answer: broken chaparral branches all pointing one way—northward. He smiled. A hungry boy would follow his nose. Only wagons consistently heading in one direction would break branches like that—they would be heading for home.

Jack rode slowly for a while, feeling the new warmth of day and studying the land ahead. Near the foothills he caught a quick light flare where the sun struck a tin roof. He loped ahead for several miles without bothering to read sign and eventually came out into the clearing of a mine. Two men looked up from a rickety oak cart as he approached and moved out to meet him. He drew up and nodded.

"Howdy. Did a kid on a stud horse ride through here a while back?"

One of the miners grinned when he answered. "He rode through, yes."

"Did you feed him?"

"Yep, an' he ate like a bear, too."

"How long ago did he ride on?"

"Early . . . hour or so after sunup."

Jack looked toward the mountains. "By that way?"

"Yep."

"Did he have anything to say?"

"Not a hell of a lot. Only that he was heading east looking for work." The miner smiled. " 'Course, he was headin' north all the time."

The second miner came closer. "Run off with his paw's stud horse, did he?" he asked with amusement.

"Something like that," Jack answered.

"Quite a horse, too. Only now he's a mite lame . . . walkin' on eggs. The kid should've got him shod first."

Jack agreed. "He's getting pretty tender all right."

The miner's twinkle lingered. "Not as tender as the kid's backsides'll be when his old man catches up to him, I reckon."

Both the miners laughed. Jack asked how Rob was holding up and the first miner shrugged.

"That game leg's botherin' him a mite. Outside o' that he's holdin' up all right."

The second miner sobered. "Touchy about that leg," he said. "I was fixin' to help him down . . . he give me one hell of a dirty look and got down by himself."

Jack slacked off the reins and nodded. "Much obliged," he said, and lifted the chestnut into a lope and held him to it until he was dark with sweat, then he alternated between a standing trot and a fast walk, cooling him out. Then more loping until the road into the mountains switched back, almost meeting itself near the summit of a ridge. There Jack stopped, put both hands on the saddle horn, and bent forward, blocking in squares of countryside seeking movement.

Ridge after ridge of rocky upthrusts lay, blue and heat-hazed, as far as he could see. Through them the old road wound, yellow, showing briefly clinging to a slope, then plunging deep into timbered cañons to struggle upward again, always working its way northwesterly toward the horizon.

He got down, made a cigarette, and smoked it leisurely while the sun climbed steadily higher. Smoked and never looked away, knowing sooner or later movement would show in all that stillness, when Rob would come working his way out of some gloomy cañon or through some dark spit of trees.

Then he saw him, a dark speck far ahead, moving slowly over the dusty roadway. He watched him stop where a freshet gushed from a hillside, water the tired stud horse, and sit wearily and dejected in the warming light.

He got up, mounted, shook out the reins, and set his horse toward the claybank road. He made a little better time than he should have in that rugged country but he wanted to close the distance before afternoon shadows came. Later, he sniffed the air to make certain it was blowing away from him. He did not want the stud horse to scent his mount and whinny.

The distance closed swiftly. Jack reined down to a fast walk, watching ahead to avoid rocks—anything that would sound under a steel shoe and warn of his coming. The only sound he made was of rubbing leather.

He came at last to a buck run and pushed his horse up it. From the ridge he paused briefly to admire the smoky view and blow his mount, then he started down the far side. Ahead, he could hear the rush of falling water. Where he rejoined the road a long-spending curve separated him from the ridge and the spring. He rode around it on a loose rein. Rob did not sense him until the stud horse snorted. Then he started violently and sprang up, one hand white-knuckled around the pistol butt at his waistband.

Jack drew up, let the reins hang, gazed down, and nodded. "You made pretty good time," he said.

The boy's face filled with dark color and he said nothing.

Jack looked at Merton's stud horse. "Too bad he wasn't shod. You'd have been out of the county by now."

Puzzled because the big man had come from the north, Rob asked: "How did you get here?"

"Followed you." The man grinned wryly. "If I'd been you, I'd have stayed down around that glass-rock country. You could see anyone trailing you and hide from them." He swung down, stood hip-shot in the roadway, watching the boy. "Well, it's all over now."

Rob's nostrils quivered. "I'm not going back," he said with vehemence.

Jack shrugged. "If you don't, it'll mean the others'll catch you farther on. You can't hope to escape them on a sore-footed horse, Rob."

"What others?"

"Your uncle's crew from rail's end. They're behind us somewhere. You lost 'em at the glass rock but by now they'll have worked around it and found either your tracks or mine."

The blue eyes were unblinkingly on the big man. "I can't go back."

"Sure doesn't seem that simple now, does it?" Jack's gaze dropped a little. "Is that the gun you were going to bring me?"

The boy looked down and touched the weapon. "Yes." He looked up again. "You want it, Jack?"

"No, you keep it for now, son." He paused a moment, then said: "You can't solve anything with it, Rob."

"I could've gotten away, though."

"Naw, not really. What you were running from isn't that easy to evade. What was it? Cavin . . . your uncle? You'd have found others just like them somewhere else. Then you'd have had to run

119

again and pretty soon you'd be doing nothing but running."

"I don't want a sermon," the boy said bitterly. "I'd have started fresh somewhere else . . . where I wasn't known."

Jack watched the stud horse nuzzle the spring water. "Why?" he asked mildly. "What's wrong with Herd? Don't blame it on the town, Rob. You know something? I came a long way to settle in Herd, and I've seen lots of towns in my time."

"But you're big and strong."

"Let me finish," Jack said. "No matter where you go, you'll always remember Herd. For one thing your folks are there."

"Dead."

"All right, dead. But they're there and no other place'd have the same meaning for you. So . . . the thing you've got to do is face up to whatever's in Herd you don't like. Face up to it like a man would, Rob . . . like I'd do . . . and prove to yourself in your own eyes that you're a man."

"I can't, Jack."

"Listen, Rob, every time you run away from something, you just become that much more of a coward . . . to yourself. Maybe no one else'll ever know you're a coward but you'll know it, and that's what counts, believe me."

The thin face lifted. It was wan, drawn, and tired-looking. "I don't have to be a coward. The next place I come to I can stay in."

Jack shook his head. "No you couldn't. You'd just stay until someone said . . . 'I don't believe I can use a cripple in my shop . . . ,' then you'd be off again. You'd be running from something you'll probably never escape from. See, Rob?"

"It isn't that. It's my uncle. He hates me. I know he does. Before my grandpaw died, the other kids used to play with me a little. Now they don't. My uncle told Mister Cavin not to let them." The blue eyes changed, became hard. "But if they knew I'd outridden a posse. . . ."

"You didn't outride it, though."

"All but you."

"Don't you think I'm part of it, Rob?"

"No, you wouldn't be riding with my uncle's men."

Jack squatted in the roadway, picked up a pine needle, and broke off small segments of it. "No," he said slowly, "I'm not part of your uncle's posse. But I'm going to take you back just the same. Rob, it's got to be that way."

The sound of gusty breathing made the man look up. Rob was struggling to hold back hot-welling tears. "What did I ever do to you?" he demanded.

"Nothing. I'm not thinking about me, I'm thinking about you."

"What is there about me that makes everything turn out . . . bad . . . always?"

Jack snapped the last of the pine needle and dropped it. "It's not you, Rob, it's life. Sometimes

121

it seems like some of us get more'n our share of misery."

"Why? What have I ever done?"

"Well, folks'll tell you things happen like they do so's you'll grow up to be a better man," Jack said, recalling words from his own youth, words he didn't believe were right.

Rob shook his head on the verge of tears. "I didn't ever want to lose my mother or my dad or my grandpaw. I didn't want to be a better man. I don't want to grow up to be one now."

Jack sat with the sun across his shoulders, listening to the crashing silence and wishing mightily Amy Southard were there to put the things into words that he was thinking. He took out his tobacco sack, made a cigarette, and lit it. Then let it lie between his fingers until it went out. Finally, as the shadows lengthened, he cast it aside and stood up.

"Let's start back, Rob."

"No!"

Thin shoulders shook in silent anguish.

"Rob, I've been thinking. I reckon I sort of let you down. I didn't mean to. I figured you were going to learn a trade. Well, seems your uncle had other notions. Now I want to tell you this . . . only a plain damned fool makes the same mistake twice, and I don't think I'm a damned fool. Come on, we'll go back and things'll be different. I promise you that."

"How can they be different . . . back there . . . in Herd?"

Jack mounted his horse and sat there, watching the boy limp toward the weary stud horse. "We'll make 'em be different," he said.

Rob wriggled up the side of the stud horse and settled into the saddle. When Jack started down the road, he followed. They had traveled perhaps a mile when Jack looked around. Rob's face was dry but the pain and hurt were still there.

"First thing we got to do," the man said, "is get that stud horse back where he belongs."

VI

The next time the big man looked back, the boy had a hand on the crest of the stud horse's neck. He saw Jack watching him and said: "He's sore-footed."

"Yeah, I know. I saw that from the way he was walking when I was tracking you." Jack grinned. "You'd make a mighty poor horse thief. You'd make a lot better saddle maker."

They rode a while in silence before the boy spoke again: "Where'll we go?"

"Why, back to town."

"I mean after we get back there."

Jack settled deeper into the saddle. "To the shop, I reckon," he said with no conviction. He began to frown.

As they rode south, furred with the dust of travel, the big man's determination grew. He had no plan—had never had one beyond finding the boy and the stolen horse—but one thing he was certain of—Rob was not going back to Cavin's shack.

They topped out over a knoll, barren and scrubbed clean by endless winds. There, Jack drew up to study the long breadth of land below them. There were shades of gray—sage, chaparral, buckbrush—and bursts of dark greenery. It all lay vividly clear beneath the weight of fading day. Even the square specks far ahead where the mine was, where the downward march of forest ended and the plain began, was limned with crystal clarity.

There was no wind, no sound, and no stirring. Later, when they were moving again, Jack halted once to sniff and look upward where a stealing grayness was infiltrating the atmosphere. The air had become coarse and the sky had taken on a leadenness, its distended belly low. In this threatening late afternoon environment the man and boy were silhouetted against the upland darkness, moving lower toward the flat land, where trees and brush were dwarfed by distance and the world was splashed with ragged shades of color below gray-scudding clouds. Later, when they were near the plains, the lop-sided old moon arose over all this, a blaze of silver in the stillness.

A hushed breeze ran fetlock-high through the dust of the roadway, making a sighing sound as it threaded its way over near edges and plunged downward, out along the desert.

Jack heard it, felt its residue along his legs, and smelled its roiled mustiness strong with rain fragrance. He watched its fingerlings twine up through his horse's mane.

There was an everlasting sameness to this country, an eternal patience that permeated everything. Some of it went into him as he rode along, watching for movement, for sign of Logan's railroaders.

He looked around at the thin face beside him, saw its drawn and tired look, and, when they were back down on the desert floor, moving through warmer air, he stopped for a rest once they hit the road. It ran torpidly crooked with a rare glint of stones along its course, like snakeskin markings.

Then, when they were moving again, they angled away from the road so as to miss the mine. Jack held to a southeasterly course, weaving his way over land swells and beyond the rolls and hollows of the foothills until they were far to the rear.

The brush became heavier on the route Jack was taking, and the stud horse wince-stepped whenever he walked on stones he could no longer see to avoid. They worked their way through the brush with only heads and shoulders showing. It may have been a needless precaution but Jack took it anyway. He did not mean for them to be found.

Once, crossing an open space, Rob said: "That's sure a nice chestnut horse, isn't he?"

"Yep," Jack agreed offhandedly. "He's good."

"We could use a horse like him . . . couldn't we?"

Jack looked down at his mount, then around to the boy. He smiled slowly. "I'll be blessed if I know what for," he said. "But I expect we could."

"Jack?"

"Yeah."

"I been practicing with the gun. Do you want to see how good I am with it?"

"Not right now, son. No sense in telling the world we're out here."

The sky became darker, the air warmer, and the night perfectly still.

They had been riding steadily for two hours after leaving the mountains when a flat-sounding rifle shot echoed in the hush.

Jack jerked his horse to a halt. Rob's animal, following too closely, bumped him. The boy's voice was sharp. "Wasn't that a shot, Jack?"

"Sure was." Jack listened a moment, then shook out his reins. "Probably your uncle's men signaling to one another. Anyway, whoever made it was a long way off."

"Yeah. Maybe it's my uncle's men an' they see it's going to rain and want to head for Herd."

The big man nodded and they started out again.

"Will we get caught in the rain, Jack?"

"I suppose so, Rob. If we could go by the road maybe we wouldn't . . . maybe we could hit town before she busts loose. But we can't go by the road."

They continued to forge ahead through the night, moving as though distance existed only to be crossed. Eventually Jack reined clear of the brush patches and kept to open country. The air smelled of brimstone. The moon began to look hazy and swollen. It shone off a broad field of obsidian ahead.

"There's your glass rock," Jack said, pointing.

Rob's reply was small. "Golly, we're close to the Merton place, aren't we?"

"Yep."

They made a wide circle of Percy Merton's pasture. Jack was sitting very erect in the saddle now, alert and listening. Once, the stud horse nickered. Rob see-sawed the reins and cut him off. Then Jack swung down, beckoned for Rob to dismount, handed him the chestnut's reins, and started forward into the night afoot leading the stud horse. He said nothing.

The corral loomed up. Jack off-saddled, turned the stud horse in, closed the pole gate, and tossed the bridle on the ground near the saddle. The stud horse went down in the dust and rolled. Then he stood up, wide-legged and shook all over. Finally, as Jack was hastening away, he threw up his head and let off a piercing whistle. Jack stopped and turned, saw a lantern appear in the middle distance, over by Merton's house, and hurried to where Rob was waiting. He swung up, helped Rob into position behind the cantle, and rode away. The lantern was bobbing rapidly in the direction of the pole corral.

Rob said: "What'll he do, Jack?"

"Find his horse, son. That's about all he can do this time of night."

They rode southward for a long time. There was nothing but the muffled scuff of the chestnut's hoof falls to break the silence. Then the boy spoke again, his voice small.

"I'm scairt, Jack."

"Sure you are. You were scairt when you took the stud horse. And I expect you were scared out on the desert last night."

"No, not last night I wasn't. But I sure was when I was saddling the stud horse."

"We'll be back pretty quick and there won't be much to be scared of."

"Yes there will . . . my uncle."

"Maybe he won't find you."

"Yes he will. And he'll make me go back, too."

Thin hands tightened on the big man's upper arms.

Jack looked ahead. He could not see the town yet but it was there. Thinking of Josh Logan, he said: "If he sends you back to Cavin's, he's going to have to work at it, son."

"Maybe we ought to go by Amy's place. She's smart . . . for a girl."

"And pretty," Jack added.

"Yeah. Smart an' pretty."

"Who's her paw, Rob?"

"He's dead. I guess he must have died when she was little . . . like my paw did. She lives with her mother. Sheriff Farmer's her uncle."

Jack craned his neck for a backward squint. "Sheriff Farmer . . . her uncle?"

"That's what she told me. He's her mother's brother."

The boy's grip tightened briefly, then he pointed ahead with one hand.

"There are the lights, Jack."

Herd lay on their right, easterly, a dark, faint series of humps and squares against the night. Jack kept on until he was at the outskirts, then he cut into an alleyway and rode down it almost to the rear opening of Buck's barn. There he halted, got down, and helped Rob down.

"You stay here a minute," he told the boy. "I'll get rid of the horse, then we'll go to the shop."

Rob nodded. The big man walked off, leading the chestnut gelding, and Rob faded deeper into the gloom, waiting.

Where an orange oblong of light lay across the alleyway, Jack halted, off-saddled, unbridled, and flagged the tired horse up into the barn. He then put the tack inside the door and turned back. A big fat raindrop struck the earth at his feet with an audible sound. He paused, looked up, then moved on.

He and Rob crossed through the Stygian darkness down a way from the lighted section of town, got into the alleyway leading to the saddle shop, and made their way to the rear door. The raindrops were falling more frequently now and the wind was rising. Jack opened the door, moved aside for Rob to pass through, then looked back at the empty alleyway. There was nothing there; no shadows that shaped up, but he hadn't really expected there to be. He entered, closed and bolted the door, and turned forward. The little room was as dark as the inside of a well. From a way off Rob's voice came, timid-sounding and small.

"I thought we were goin' t' see Amy."

"It's pretty late," Jack replied. "Maybe in the morning."

"Oh. Jack? Could we eat something?"

The big man smiled in the darkness. "I reckon so," he said, "providing you can find your mouth in the dark. No point in advertising that we're back by lighting the lamps."

They ate in darkness, listening to the rainstorm come, wave after wave of increasing wind and water. The building quivered under the impact.

Finally Jack showed Rob where the bunk was and waited until the boy was snuggled down under the quilts. By then the storm was spending its full fury against the town.

"Jack, here's the gun."

The man took it, hefted it unconsciously, then put it on a high shelf and turned away. From the bed a tired, thickening voice said: "Aren't you going to bed?"

"Yeah, directly. Right now I'm going out into the shop for a smoke. Good night, Rob."

"Good night."

The shop's front window was streaked and blurred. Beyond it wavy paths of lamplight fell against the glistening roadway. Jack made a cigarette, smoked it standing motionlessly by the cutting table looking out. He was straightening up to turn away when a shapeless form darkened the window, then moved along to the door and rapped sharply on it.

It was Buck. He had obviously dressed in haste and his lined old face was puffy from sleep. He sputtered and shook off water as he squeezed past the open door and turned to face the big man.

Jack closed and locked the door. Without turning, he said: "That was pretty good timing, Buck."

"Wasn't no accident," the liveryman shot back. "I left word for the hostler to let me know the second you brought the horse back."

"I see."

"Did you bring him back, too?"

"The boy? Sure." Jack motioned Buck toward a stool. "Sit down," he said, and went back by the cutting table. "Where's Logan?"

"Out lookin' for his railroaders."

"I hope he gets drenched."

"You got a lamp in here?"

"Sure. But I don't aim to light it."

Buck's crooked, gnomish figure drew up suddenly and his voice went high. "You ain't got him here, have you?"

"Couldn't leave him out in the rain, could I?"

"Dammit, Jack, this's the first place Logan'll look when he gets back."

"I can't help that."

"Listen, boy, you can't have the lad here. That'd be all Logan would need to nail you to a cross. He's already as sore as the devil chasin' a crippled saint." Buck cocked his head suddenly. "I've got it. We'll hide him at my barn."

Jack leaned on the table. "And if he's found there," he said, "what'll they do to you?"

"Less chance of him bein' found there than here," Buck said stoutly.

"No. Nothing doing. Logan's down on me . . . that's all right. We'll let it stand like that. No sense in getting him down on you, too."

"It's about time someone else got mixed up in this thing," the old man insisted. "You don't think I got out of bed and come down here just to give

132

you hell about keepin' one of my horses out this long, do you?"

"What do you mean, Buck?"

"Logan's got a warrant out for your arrest . . . that's what I mean. That's why I wanted to know the second you came back. So's I could warn you to saddle up and get." Buck groped for the stool, sank down on it, and leaned forward, looking up. "Just who d'you think's going to look out for the boy after you're gone?"

The big man was still so long Buck didn't think he was going to answer at all. Then he said: "I'm not going anywhere."

"What! Are you plumb loco? Logan'll land on you like a ton of bricks." The old man squirmed. "Dammit, boy, when Logan serves that warrant, you'll be out of circulation . . . maybe for a long time. Don't you see? Whether you run or stay, you're going to be out of it, and someone's got to mind the boy."

Jack growled: "Quit hollering. I can hear you all right."

Buck subsided. He slumped on the stool and ran a coat sleeve along under his nose, then he perked up again. "Now, listen, Jack, I don't know whether this is true or not and I don't care . . . but there's a rumor around that you're an ex-convict from Yuma."

The big man's gaze fastened on the liveryman's face. He said nothing.

"If that's so, and you're arrested, you aren't going to be locked up for a day or two. You'll be taken away. What happens to Rob then?"

"I'm not in jail yet."

"Use your head," Buck retorted, voice rising again. "Hoyt Farmer'll have you by noon tomorrow. I know he looks sleepy and slow-witted, but he ain't. I've known Hoyt Farmer twenty years and there ain't a shrewder lawman in Arizona. As soon as he thinks you're back, he'll come a-lookin' for you, and believe me when Hoyt Farmer commences lookin' he never quits."

Jack gestured tiredly. "All right. Suppose you hide Rob . . . and get found out?"

"Who's goin' to find out?"

"Logan, that's who. If you think Farmer's smart, let me tell you that Logan's twice as smart. Who's been my closest friend since I came to Herd? You. Who's been outspokenly against Josh Logan? You."

"All right!" Buck exclaimed. "Let him suspect me. Let him come an' look. He won't find nothin' at all. You just leave that to me. I didn't just come down in this here rain, y'know. I been around a long time an' I know my way around a little, too. Logan be damned." Buck got off the stool and raised a hand. "And another thing, Jack, you got to leave tonight . . . right now."

"Why?"

"Because this here rain'll hide your tracks, that's why. Even Hoyt Farmer won't be able to track you after a rain."

Jack's mouth quirked upward slightly in approval. "No," he stated slowly. "I guess you didn't come down in this rain. I guess you've done a little track hiding in your time."

"Never mind that," the old man replied tartly. "Let's move the kid to my hayloft while it's still darker'n pitch out."

They got Rob, quilts and all, and carried him, half asleep, across the empty, shimmering, and rain-drenched roadway and into Buck's barn. There, while the old man kept his night hawk in the harness room, Jack put the boy in the hayloft. Bedded him down well on the far side of the hay and left him.

When he descended the loft ladder, Buck was waiting. Jack beat chaff off his trousers and looked up with a head wag.

"That's the first place Logan'll look," he said.

"Yeah? Well, he won't find nothin'. Now come on, let's get you a horse. It'll be daylight in another two, three hours."

"It's not that late," the younger man said, following Buck toward the rear stalls, down near the alley entrance.

The old man stopped, drew out his watch, flicked it open, and squinted downward. "Four-thirty," he said. "It's even later'n I thought."

"Where'd the night go?" Jack asked, surprised at the lateness.

Buck was reaching for a stall door when he said: "They got a habit of just lastin' eight hours. Here, put this bridle on him and I'll fetch the saddle."

"Buck?"

"Yes?"

"There's something I've got to do before I leave."

"I can guess," the old man grumbled. "You got to see Amy Southard." He started for the harness room. "Go ahead and see her . . . just be gone before sunup."

By the time Buck returned with the saddle Jack had led the horse out into the alleyway where a wet wind was running. The overhead sound of rain was loud and steady.

As the old man heaved the saddle up, he grunted: "There's a slicker tied behind the cantle. You'd best put it on now." As an afterthought he added: "It's a black one . . . not yellow."

Jack got the slicker, shrugged into it, and reached for the reins Buck was holding out. For a moment they looked into each other's eyes, then the old man cleared his throat and spat aside.

"Now, listen, boy. There's a little juniper and oak knoll three miles east of town on the Lighthill Grade. It's the only knoll around there with trees on it. I'll either bring you some grub up there or send you some by noon tomorrow . . . I mean today. If there's any news, I'll put a note with it."

Buck sighed. "After that, though, you'd best leave the country. And . . . don't write me no letters. At least not for a couple of weeks. You understand?"

"Listen, Buck, I'm not leaving the country. I'll hide out for a few days but I'm not. . . ."

"You idiot! Logan'll have posses all over the place!"

"Let him. I didn't come down in this rain, either. I've ducked posses before. The thing is I can't leave you with the short end of the rope."

"Jack, you damned fool. I've got. . . ."

"There's another thing, too, Buck. I can't run out . . . not after telling the boy that a man doesn't run from his troubles, he faces up to them."

Buck's mouth remained open. A long rush of air came out of it. His shoulders slumped a little, then he made a weary hand motion. "All right, son. All right. You do what you think's right . . . and I'll do what I can . . . and I expect the rest of it's up to the Big Spirit." Buck's jaw thrust out. "Now git!"

VII

Jack rode through the driving rain as far as the Southard place. There, while his horse stood humped up against the cold, he went up to the door and knocked. It seemed an eternity before an elderly woman answered. She was holding a blue-black revolver in one hand. He affected not to see it.

"Could I see Miss Amy for just a moment," he asked. "It's important, ma'am, or I wouldn't be here at this hour of the morning."

The older woman studied his face a long time before turning away. "I'll get her," she said, then the girl's voice, unmistakable, came from the gloom beyond.

"Who is it, Mother?"

"A young man, honey. He wants to talk to you."

Amy pulled the door open wider and peered out. She had a voluminous blue wrapper around her. She reached out suddenly and pulled at Jack's sleeve. He resisted.

"I'm wet and muddy," he said. "Besides, this won't take long." He held out a key and an envelope. "The key's to my saddle shop. You keep it. In this envelope is eleven hundred dollars. You keep that, too."

"But, Jack. . . ."

"Let me finish. I got Rob. He's in hiding at Buck's barn. I've got to disappear for a spell until his uncle's cooled down. Miss Amy, you and Buck and I are the only friends that kid's got. You use that money to keep his uncle from getting him . . . use it any way you have to or any way you want to. The shop . . . well, if the money runs out, sell it and use that money, too."

"You're . . . running . . . away?"

He saw the disbelief in her face and drew in a big breath. "I'm an ex-convict, Miss Amy."

She murmured something that sounded like—"I know."—but he wasn't sure what it was and he didn't give her a chance to repeat it.

"Logan can frame me back into prison. He once told me how easily he could do it. Well, that's why I'm leaving now. I'm not running . . . not away, anyway. I'll be back. All I'm asking of you is a little help . . . for a time."

The words trailed off. Beyond Amy her mother stood rock-like with the pistol in her hand. She seemed to be an aged duplicate of the girl. A big gust of wind tore at the roof of the porch and hurried on. Amy took a big breath, reached for the key and envelope, and held them without looking away from the big man's face.

"All right, Jack, all right. But I think you're wrong. I don't think Josh Logan could railroad you."

He shook his head with impatience. "Listen, all Logan has to do is have witnesses testify in court they've seen me wearing a gun. That's all. It's against the law for ex-felons to pack guns, Miss Amy."

"But you've never carried a gun in Herd. The people could swear to that."

"You still don't understand," he said a trifle sharply. "Logan could have ten of his railroaders swear they saw me armed. That's all it'd take to send me back to Yuma. He'd do it. I know he would."

He shook his hat, struck his slickered leg with it, and put it back on his head. Amy moved across the porch and stopped close, looking up into his face.

"Jack, you're not running out, are you? You're not being frightened off . . . ?"

He made a bitter smile. "Amy, I don't scare worth a damn. That's been one of my troubles. No, I haven't begun to fight back yet. All I need now is a little time. I'm relying on you and Buck to help me get that by keeping Logan away from Rob." He reached out and touched her. "I've really got no right to get you involved, though, have I?"

She took his hand and squeezed it. "You're not getting me involved. I'm the one that dragged you into this." She let his hand go and stepped back. "You can trust me, Jack. I'll do everything that can be done."

He touched his hat to them both and turned away. Wet earth squished underfoot as he went back to the horse, swung up, and rode northerly out of town through the wind and rain.

By the time he got to the easterly cut-off the day was paling in the east and the rain was diminishing. By the time he located Buck's tree-topped little knoll, steel gray morning was close. He topped the little hill, rode into the screen of dripping trees, got down, and took off the slicker. The rain was passing, only a heavy mist remained, and, as daylight grew, the desert warmed up.

He tied the slicker behind the cantle, then made a leisurely reconnaissance of the land around Buck's hill. A mile beyond, hidden from the knoll by a square-hewn granite bluff, was Logan's railroad camp. He rode there, got down, and rolled a cigarette, watching the men and the camp below the ridge.

Rain had of course slowed the railroaders' progress. A freshly laid roadbed ran out ahead of the steel ribbons, which came out of the northeast, and terminated where shacks, Sibley tents, and an army of wagons stood. Men were working down there, but half-heartedly; the ground was too wet to do much. A span of mules came from the west, probably from a tie camp back in the mountains, laden with squared logs. Profanity from the teamster rose into the air. The mules slithered, chain harness rattled, and section hands, turning to watch the wagon's progress, called encouragement. Finally, when the wagon halted beyond the steel lines, dozens of men went forward to unload the ties. While they were working, a small work engine puffed up, pushing four flatcars laden with gleaming steel, new track rails. A mounted man came from behind the shacks and bellowed orders. Most of the section hands left the wagon and went back to unload the flatcars.

There was smoke rising from a black pipe in the center of Logan's camp. Jack surmised the big tent where this came from was the mess hall. Far out, a goodly distance from the other residences, stood a small, square hut with a bright red door. The powder cache. For a long time Jack's gaze lingered here. Finally, satisfied that he had seen all there was to see, the big man stubbed out his cigarette, mounted the horse, and headed back toward the far knoll. It was close to midday by then and the sun was just beginning to break through the overcast.

He hadn't been there an hour when a moving speck coming from the direction of Herd caught and held his attention. The rider turned east at the cut-off and headed straight for the knoll. He was too far away to identify, but he wasn't so far away that Jack didn't move his horse back farther into the trees, and remain with him, watching.

The stranger rode past the knoll and Jack relaxed, thinking he was a railroader going to the camp. Then he left the road and made a big half circle of the knoll, and uneasiness touched the big man. Clearly the stranger was studying the wet earth for tracks—and just as surely he would find them.

He did. He found Jack's tracks going toward the granite ridge and returning. He stopped, stoked up a pipe, lit it, puffed up a head of smoke, then shook out his reins, heading straight for the hilltop.

It would be useless to flee. The oncoming rider

would be able to see him easily if he rode down off the hill, and, since the stranger was armed and Jack was not, pursuit could only end one way.

Jack found a stout oak limb, leaned it against the white-oak tree he was using for cover, and waited until the stranger got to the top of his hill.

There was something familiar about the stranger's horse, and even about the relaxed, easy way the armed man sat the saddle, but until he reined up and swung his head in a slow study of the knoll and the trees where Jack was watching, he hadn't recognized him. Now he did. It was Sheriff Hoyt Farmer. The badge on his coat and the hat-shadowed roughness of his face showed at the same time.

The sheriff knocked dottle from his pipe, stowed it in a coat pocket, thumbed back his black hat, and called softly: "Swift?"

Echoes came back from the trees but there was no answer. For a while Sheriff Farmer sat perfectly still, then, very methodically and almost as though he were sighing from the effort, he swung out and down, bent a long look at the ground, and started forward. Jack knew his tracks would betray him, and, resigned to being arrested, he stepped out into plain sight. It was the movement that halted Hoyt Farmer. He looked up slowly, rocked his head slightly to one side, and nodded.

"Guess you didn't hear me call," he said mildly.

Jack came forward. "I heard you," he replied.

The sheriff nodded. "Sure," he said, and turned toward his horse. "Amy sent you some vittles."

Jack watched the sheriff take a tied bundle from his saddle and walk forward with it. He made no move toward the gun at his hip, nor did his unwavering, deceptively drowsy gaze look other than friendly.

Jack accepted the bundle and spoke at the same time. "The way I heard it Logan has a warrant."

"He had it. And I reckon he wanted to serve it himself, too. But this morning it's no good."

"What do you mean?"

"Well, to start with, that warrant was only good for twenty-four hours. To finish with, after Logan heard that you'd left the country . . . alone . . . he threw the warrant away."

"If he thought I'd left the country, how come you're here?"

"*He* thought you'd left. I didn't."

Jack went to a deadfall and sat down. While he ate, Sheriff Farmer lit his pipe again and smoked, admiring the way afternoon sunlight flashed and sparkled off the damp countryside. After a while he faced Jack and spoke. "Y'know, Logan's still lookin' for Rob."

"Is he?"

"Yep. He doesn't even know Merton's stud horse come back, unsaddled himself, and put himself back in the corral."

Jack saw the faint twinkle in Hoyt Farmer's eyes. He continued to eat and said nothing. The sheriff went to the deadfall and sank down beside Swift.

"Damnedest thing," he said. "You try an' keep a secret and folks'll find it out before you can say scat. You sort of bungle things, like finding the kid and putting the stud horse back, and folks don't pay much attention." Sheriff Farmer cleaned his pipe stem with a stalk of dead grass. "Maybe folks're more influenced by the way they feel, than by the way they *should* feel. You reckon, Swift?"

"I don't know what you're talking about, Sheriff."

"Maybe you don't." The sheriff finished cleaning his pipe and puffed contentedly. "The thing is, Herd's a small town. Folks take sides on just about every issue. And being human, I expect they're pretty much influenced by what they see . . . not what's legal or illegal."

Jack finished eating, folded the cloth on his leg very carefully, smoothed out each wrinkle, and held it out. "Tell Amy I'm obliged, will you?"

"Sure. She'll be glad to know that, too. Now . . . as I was saying . . . folks around Herd are pretty fair judges . . . not about what's right according to law, but about what's right by human understanding."

Jack made a cigarette, lit it, and exhaled. He

bent a long, ironic stare at the sheriff. "It's sure taking you a long time to shake out your loop," he said.

Sheriff Farmer straightened up on the log. "I guess it is at that. But it's that kind of a day. A feller likes to sort of ruminate now and then. The older I get, the more of it I do." He looked squarely at Jack. "There's a lot of feeling in town, Swift. Folks couldn't help but see how Logan's hurt the kid an' how you stuck up for him. They favor you over Logan. That's about what it adds up to."

"I see. Well, it's good to know, sure, but it doesn't help the kid much."

"How about you?"

Jack shrugged. "I'll get by. I always have."

Farmer pocketed his pipe and looked thoughtful. "Not without a gun you won't . . . not this time."

"What do you mean?"

"This. In simple language, Swift, you're a sitting duck. You've crossed Josh Logan. I've never yet seen anyone do that and stay healthy. His own brother crossed him. . . ."

Jack felt a sudden jar. He stared at the lawman. "Go on."

Farmer looked away. "Nothing much more worth saying."

"Why did you mention Logan's brother?"

"The summer after he crossed Josh he died."

"Sure. In a flash flood," Jack said. "Flash floods happen."

146

"They sure do," Farmer replied, getting to his feet and stretching mightily. "Well, I expect I'd better get back to town." He dropped his arms and looked down. "Where's the kid?"

Jack got up, too. He didn't answer the sheriff's question. The other thing was still on his mind. He studied Hoyt Farmer's serenely impassive face. He would get nothing from the sheriff that Farmer was not willing to volunteer. But he could try.

"The way you said that . . . about Logan's brother. . . ."

"Forget it. It stuck in my craw for a long time. Coincidence is one thing. Too much coincidence is another. That's all there was to it. You can't talk your way around a flash flood. It's an act of Nature and Josh Logan or nobody else could direct it or predict it. Nature just happened along to do Josh's killing for him." Farmer looked out where his horse was drowsing. "Now tell me where you got the kid hid?"

"I don't have him hidden."

"But you found him."

"Yes."

"And you put the stud horse back."

"Yes."

Farmer ran a hand under his jaw and sighed. "And you know where the kid is, too." He turned. Jack traded stares with him without answering. The sheriff nodded. "I'm going to give you a little unofficial advice . . . for Amy's sake, you understand . . . get yourself a gun if you figure to stay around Herd. If you don't figure to stay . . . don't waste another day being on your way."

"I'm going to stay."

Sheriff Farmer's voice dropped slightly. His eyes brightened with irony. "And the gun?" he asked softly.

Jack understood both the tone and the look. He smiled without mirth. "You know I can't pack a gun."

For a time Farmer said nothing, then he slumped, stood with his weight balanced on one leg. And he frowned. "Yeah, I know . . . Yuma." He continued to frown. "Swift, you're walking right into it. You know that, don't you? Logan'll know the kid's been found by tonight. If he finds him, you can get away . . . probably . . . and he might not try to find you. If he doesn't find him . . . he'll have your scalp."

"I know."

Farmer looked up quickly. "What're you going to do about it?"

"I'm staying, Sheriff, and, if Logan gets my topknot, he's going to earn it."

"You got a plan?"

"I've got one. I just thought of it."

Farmer waited patiently but Jack said no more and finally the sheriff turned and walked to his horse. After mounting, he said: "Better change your rendezvous. Right now you're not wanted, so what you do is none of my business. But if Logan swears out another warrant . . . and I expect he will . . . it'll be my job to find you and bring you in."

"Thanks," Jack said roughly. "And tell Amy thanks, too."

Farmer reined toward the road. "I'll do that," he said.

Jack watched him ride down to the road, swing west, and grow small in the sparkling distance. He continued to study the land toward Herd for a long time. Except for some distant, crawling wagons, there was no traffic.

The sun sank lower, Jack smoked a cigarette, lost in thought, then he got his horse, mounted, and started toward town. Long before he got close the shadows were lengthening. It was going to be a pleasantly warm night; he could tell from the high warmth of a clear sky.

He had to see Buck. As the sheriff had said, it was no longer safe for him to use the hilltop near Logan's camp for his hide-out. If Farmer had tracked him there, so could others.

Herd stood out, rain-washed and vivid, in the dusk. He angled westerly to hit the alleyway leading to Buck's barn and made the last hundred yards on foot. Fortunately the old man was tallying sacked grain at the rear of the barn when Jack came out of the shadows of the alley. He sucked in a quick, sharp breath of air and pulled the big man deeper into the shadows.

"You daft, comin' here tonight? Boy, Logan's just found out that the kid's been found."

"How could he know that?"

"Simple. You talked to some miners when you was lookin' for him. They told Logan's men about it today right here in town. They even seen you an' the kid comin' down out o' the hills."

"Oh."

"Oh, hell," Buck said, greatly agitated. "Logan's got another warrant out for you for stealin' his nephew. Hoyt Farmer took a posse out about half an hour ago, lookin' for you."

Jack grunted. "He won't get me." When Buck continued to spout, Jack told him of the meeting with Sheriff Farmer on the hilltop. Buck subsided, scratched his head, and screwed up his face.

"Well," he said. "That beats hell. Now, why'd Hoyt do that for you?"

Jack smiled. "Amy," he said.

Buck considered this and finally agreed. Then he said: "But you got to light out, son. An' this time don't come back."

"We've got to have another rendezvous, Buck."

"All right. You name it and that's where it'll be, but you got to leave, an' right now."

"Do you know where that glass rock is, west of the Merton place?"

"Sure I know."

"I'll be there waiting."

Buck looked puzzled. "Waiting? Waiting for what?"

"For Rob. You put him on a horse and send him out there tonight."

Buck recoiled. For a second he was stonily silent, then he began to swear. "Jack, I figured you had some sense. Why, Logan's men'll be watching every road from now on."

"I'm not leaving without him, Buck."

"Jack, they'll get him sure as God made green apples. Then everything'll be for nothing."

"Then I'll take him with me now," the big man insisted.

"You can't."

"Why not? You've got a horse he can ride and. . . ."

"He ain't here."

Jack turned to stone. His stare was bleak and still. Buck's face contorted. He dropped his voice to a whisper. "Amy took him to her place. She's got him hid in the attic."

VIII

Jack left Buck's barn via the alley. He went as far north as a narrow dogtrot between two buildings and beyond there emerged onto the town's main plank walk. There was some evening traffic but not much. The roadway was a quagmire of mushy gumbo. From Cardoza's Saloon midway down the square, southward, came the strident noises of an out-of-tune piano. Directly across from him was Herd's major mercantile emporium. Behind him, as yet undiscovered, was the dark and watchful silhouette of a man who had followed him from the alley behind Buck's barn.

He crossed the roadway finally and started north toward the Southard place. Where the plank walk changed, at the end of Herd's business buildings and the beginning of the residential area because the houses were farther back from the road, he made the customary right turn before the plank walk straightened out again. It was while he was navigating the drafty opening of an alleyway here that he caught sight of a moving shadow deep in the alleyway. With every reason to be cautious this fading apparition inspired him to continue on past the Southard home, walking faster, until he came to the empty, littered ground by the Cavin shack. There he turned in, skirted the darkened house, and hastened into the north-south alley beyond.

With darkness dripping on him from board fences and woodsheds, he waited. For a while there was neither sound nor movement, then he heard someone pushing across Cavin's rear yard and pressed deeper into the gloom.

A man appeared, cautiously at first, then more boldly, in the alleyway. He was straining to see. Jack stood like stone. The stranger took a few tentative steps southward then halted, drew out a

152

match, struck it, and, holding it cupped, studied the ground. Twenty feet away and motionless, Jack waited until he saw the stranger's sputtering light find his fresh tracks and turn to follow them. Then he moved with a speed rarely found in men of his size. The stranger dropped his match and whirled—but only in time to be sledged under the jaw and dropped as if pole-axed. He did not move.

Jack blew on his knuckles as he regarded the unconscious form, then he knelt swiftly, rifled the stranger's pockets until he found the railroad pass, and straightened up again. Logan was missing no bets. He had undoubtedly had men watching Buck's barn.

Jack stepped over the downed man and proceeded southward as far as the Southards' back fence. There, he entered the rear yard and moved fluidly as far as an old horse shed before stopping. Long minutes passed. Farther south and well beyond Southards' was the alley where he had seen the man shadowing him. Logan might or might not have another guard at the Southards'. He meant to take no chance.

Time passed, agonizing moments during which Jack knew the man he had stunned would have revived and gone to raise the alarm. He considered abandoning his plan, by now doubly dangerous because Logan would know he was—or had been at least in town. If Logan's railroaders had been on guard before, they would be even more fully alert now.

He longed to smoke. He also longed to see Amy Southard. Both desires were destined to go unrewarded; two men approached the Southard house from up along the front plank walk. Jack saw them pass briefly. Later he heard them pound on Mrs. Southard's front door. One of them he had recognized as Hoyt Farmer. The other he thought was Josh Logan. There was nothing left for him to do but get out of Herd as fast as he could.

When he left the Southard yard, he did not go north again, but hurried to the east-west alleyway, cut through it with more haste than caution, went directly across the roadway and to the spot where his horse was tied. There, with one foot in the stirrup, he was frozen into immobility by a sharp snippet of sound—once heard never forgotten—the cocking of a single-action revolver.

"Easy now," a husky voice said softly. "Keep your hands up on the saddle like that, Swift."

A gradual twisting of the head revealed his captor. He was a middle-size man in a rumpled windbreaker. He looked no more dangerous than a snarling dog except for the cocked pistol in his right fist.

"Who are you?" Jack demanded. "What do you want?"

"Well now," the soft-husky voice said affably.

154

"My name's Cavin. Ernie Cavin. I work for Mister Logan, an' I want the three hundred dollar reward he's got on you dead or alive." Cavin flicked the gun. "Take your hoof outen the stirrup. That's better. Now turn around where I can get a good look at you."

Jack turned and looked down into Cavin's face. It was a whisker-stubbled, liquor-reddened countenance with no depth of feeling to it one way or another. A weak face, but also a sharp-featured one.

"Five hundred if you put that gun away, turn around, and walk out of this alley," Jack said.

Cavin considered, licked his lips, then shook his head. "Nope. With Logan I got a future. With you . . . after the five hundred's gone . . . I got nothing." The gun did not sag or waver. "Where's Rob?"

"For three hundred dollars go find him."

Cavin smiled. "You ain't very smart, big feller. Logan pays dead or alive. I got a feelin' he'd rather have you dead."

"Then how would he find the kid?"

Cavin licked his lips. "I don't care whether he finds the kid or not. All I care about is the three hundred bucks."

"In that case," Jack said, "shoot."

Cavin wagged his head negatively. "I got a better idea," he said. "You just walk down to the end of the alley an' we'll go to Mister Logan's office an' wait for him. He'll twist it out of you . . . where you got the kid hid out."

Jack dug his heels into the mud and let his weight ride forward. It was a crazy thing to do in the face of a cocked pistol and a steady hand, but he had to do it.

"Go on," Cavin said, motioning with his gun hand. "Turn around an' let's go."

Jack sprang.

Cavin's reflexes were slow. He did not give the frantic tug that exploded the bullet until Jack was on him. The deafening sound shattered every vestige of the alley's stillness but it was the burst of dazzling light that blinded the big man. He had Cavin's coat with one hand when the blinding flash came. The other hand was locked around Cavin's gun wrist. He forced the gun hand down and out, then spun Cavin around and brought the arm up between Cavin's shoulder blades, wrenched until the gristle tore and Cavin screamed, and the gun fell in the churned earth at their feet. With his free hand he whirled Cavin and lashed out. Pain, like an electric shock, ran to his shoulder when his fist crashed into Cavin's jaw. The smaller, older man crumpled without a sound.

Jack stepped over the blur at his feet, vaulted into the saddle, and raced southward down the alleyway. At the rear entrance to Buck's barn he glimpsed a startled, white face, then it was lost in the gloom.

He was well south of Herd before full sight returned. He halted, examined his clothing, found shredded burned cloth where powder scorch had damaged his coat, but he was not wounded. After that he rode more slowly. Anger was growing in him, a kind of anger he had experienced only once or twice before in his life. Killing anger. He stopped finally, near the east-west turn of Herd Creek, and listened for pursuit. There was none. He made a cigarette and smoked it down to a stub, waiting. No one came. He flung the cigarette down and gathered up the reins. A man on the defensive accomplishes nothing and so far Josh Logan had had things his way, had kept Jack Swift on the run, had done it with no peril to himself.

The horse fidgeted, tired of standing. Jack ran a hand along his neck and spoke. "All right, pardner, we'll see how the boot fits on the other foot."

He rode around Herd northeasterly. When Buck's knoll showed, dark against the velvet night, and the road loomed up, he crossed the latter and put the former behind him. Ahead, dim but bulking large, was the granite ridge overlooking Logan's rail's end camp. He by-passed the ridge, too. Went out, around, and down behind the camp, left the horse, and continued on afoot as far as the powder house. There, by working boards loose with his hands, he got inside. Cases of dynamite and oilskin-wrapped coils of black fuse were neatly stacked. He took eight sticks of powder and a long length of fuse, went back to his horse, and rode as far as the granite ridge. There it took him nearly an hour to prepare the explosives.

Twinkling fitfully below him, the railroad camp was reflected in the light of many lanterns. He studied it for a while to confirm what he knew of its layout, then rode leisurely down off the ridge toward track's end.

A little wind had risen. Lanterns flickered and the canvas tops of hutments sucked in and puffed out. Jack set his charge five hundred feet behind the little work engine, tamped earth over it, lit the fuse, and rode away with a smaller bundle of sticks in his hand. As he neared the freshly piled ties, he looked back. The first fuse was spluttering closer to the dynamite; he did not have much time.

It didn't take much to set the second charge beneath the racked-up ties. After he lit this second fuse, he vaulted into the saddle and rode hard for the granite ridge. When he halted near the top, his horse was grunting from the climb. He moved forward more leisurely. By the time he was atop the ridge and well beyond harm's way, the little wind had turned into a steady blow.

When the blasts came, they were less than a minute apart. Afterward the camp was in a turmoil. Men ran forward, holding lanterns high. Others yelled for guns and horses. A few stood rooted in the mud outside their huts, staring down where splintered railroad ties were scattered. Behind the engine, where the largest charge had gone off, was a hole twenty feet deep. There the greatest cries of indignation arose; aside from having to repair the damage, the work engine could not go back for more rails until the hole had been filled and fresh track laid.

Jack did not wait any longer. He left the ridge, heading for Herd. If anything would bring Josh Logan to rail's end, this would do it.

On the outskirts of town, with the wind turned gusty again, Jack sat in the darkness smoking and waiting. It was not a long wait; four riders pushing their mounts hard came pounding out of the northeast down the roadway. Railroaders. He inhaled, smiled, and exhaled. There was no hurry; the railroaders could not rouse Sheriff Farmer and Josh Logan in less than half an hour. He dismounted, let his horse graze nearby, and found a dry place to sit and wait.

Logan was vulnerable, too vulnerable really to undertake a war of attrition against Jack Swift. If he retaliated, the only serious harm he could do Jack would be to destroy his saddle and harness shop. Jack, on the other hand, could harass the railroad camp until Logan's schedules were hopelessly delayed. There would be an investigation by the railroad company's stockholders and Logan would find himself in deep trouble.

These consoling thoughts were brief, though. He thought of Rob. He also thought of Amy and Buck. Before Josh Logan was defeated, he would strike at them, too. This sobering realization was still bothering him when he heard a number of mounted men loping northward out of town. When they passed, a quarter mile west of where he watched, he recognized only one of them— Sheriff Hoyt Farmer.

Four railroaders had entered Herd. There were nine men in the party that rode out; four would be the same railroaders who carried the news of disaster to Logan. Two more would be Logan and Hoyt Farmer. The others would be Logan's men from town, perhaps Cavin and the other railroader Jack had fought.

He got to his feet, thinking Logan could not have left many men in Herd. He went toward his horse, thinking it was a good thing. Now he could get Rob and leave. In the saddle another thought came. If he left Amy and Buck, Logan could still get his vengeance. With a black frown on his face he reined for town. Buck wouldn't leave. He knew the old man that well. He had his home, his business, and a mile-wide stubborn streak. He would never leave Herd.

And Amy, she couldn't leave without her mother. Perhaps she could, he thought, but she wouldn't. Not after placing her mother in the way of Logan's wrath.

He balled up a fist and smashed it down upon the saddle horn. He could think of no way out for all of them and bone-tiredness swept over him. He would have to get some rest and, later, some food. It was impossible to think straight right then, and after what he had done to Josh Logan he was going to need every bit of thinking power he possessed.

The wind was rising, growing stronger and warmer. He studied the sky as he approached Herd from the west. It was as clear and cloudless as glass. There would be no rain. He thought of riding to the glass-rock rendezvous but decided it was too far and headed instead for the back alley where he had met Ernie Cavin. Once there, he turned Buck's horse loose and watched it trot toward the barn with a livery animal's infallible homing instinct. Then he waited a full hour before heading toward the shadowy runway of the stable himself. The night hawk was not in sight when he slipped inside. He wanted to get to the loft and the fragrant hay beyond its overhead opening but dared not; the night hawk might come out of the harness room at any moment. He settled for an alternative and bedded down in the grain room, which was not only accessible to the back alley, but was also an easier place to escape from if the need arose.

He was asleep almost before his head hit the barley sacks. The granary was a tight little room, as dark as night and rarely visited—never at night—and usually only by Buck himself. But if it had been in the middle of Herd's main thoroughfare, he still would have slept like a stone.

Elsewhere, particularly at rail's end, there was no thought of rest. Sheriff Hoyt Farmer, surveying the damage with Josh Logan, was grimly silent. His companion, ashen with rage, scarcely heard his foreman's recitation of what had happened. Finally Logan spoke, tightly drawn lips hardly moving.

"I want that man, Sheriff. I want him killed."

Farmer's drowsy eyes raised. "What man, Logan?"

"Swift! You know *what* man as well as I do!"

The sheriff returned his gaze to the yawning hole that severed the track behind the work engine. "You got proof it was Swift, Logan?"

"Proof!" Logan roared explosively. "By God, look at that! Look at the stack of reserve ties! Ruined . . . every damned thing ruined. There's only one man who would do that and I want him. If you don't get him, I will."

Sheriff Farmer turned to gaze at the cluster of white faces around them. His glance rested briefly on Ernie Cavin and another man with a bruised jaw beside Cavin. "Hell, Logan," he said quietly. "Anyone could've done that. Swift isn't the only enemy you've got." He started to push past the listening men. "Another thing, too," he added. "You've been tryin' your darnedest to catch Swift and haven't done it, so don't tell me you'll get him if I don't."

Logan spun around. "This time I will get him. If it breaks me, I'll get him!"

Sheriff Farmer paused in mid-stride, looked long at Logan, then shook his head and continued on toward his horse.

A second man detached himself from the throng and followed along. When he and Hoyt Farmer were back where the saddled horses stood, the second man said: "You don't think it was Swift?"

"Sure it was Swift," the sheriff replied, gathering his reins and toeing into the stirrup preparatory to mounting. "But we've got to have better openers than that, Will. You've been a deputy long enough to know it."

Deputy Spencer mounted and waited for the sheriff. "I know something else, too," he said quietly. "If I was Jack Swift and had something in mind, I'd want to get Logan out of town while I did it."

The sheriff settled across his saddle and seemed to consider Spencer's words a moment, then he loosened his reins and swore. "I got a god-damned feeling we're heading for some real trouble, Will. Real trouble."

IX

Jack was awakened by loud voices beyond the granary. He straightened up, listening, then got carefully to his feet as the voices subsided and someone came toward his hiding place. As the door swung back, a dazzling shaft of daylight flooded the room from the alley and a gnome of a man entered, muttering and growling to himself. He got almost to the sacked grain before he stopped, turned very slowly, and stared up into Jack's face.

"God Almighty," Buck gasped. "You."

"You're lucky it isn't Logan," Jack said dryly.

The old man went to the door, peered up and down the barn runway, then said: "I wish it was Logan. Him I'd throw into the alley." Buck studied the beard-stubbled face a moment and some of the starch went out of him. "Well, I'll fetch you a razor an' some water. You look like hell."

As he was turning away, Jack said: "And something to eat, too."

Buck nodded and left. The big man grinned in the darkness, rubbed the back of his neck where an outraged muscle pained him, then let off a long sigh. By now Buck should have heard something.

When the old man returned—through the alley entrance, sneaking food and a wash basin into the granary—he was fairly bursting with news.

164

"Well, boy, you sure tore it this time."

"You mean the railroad camp?"

Buck put the things in his arms upon some grain sacks. "You ain't done nothing else, have you?"

"No."

"That's good," the old man said ironically. "Because Will Spencer's gone into the hills lookin' for a camp you might have there, and Hoyt Farmer took the dawn stage to Yuma."

Jack washed and shaved. "What about Rob?"

"Safer'n a bug in a rug. I saw Amy about an hour ago. We don't figure Logan suspicions her yet. He called at her house with the sheriff yesterday evenin', but she said she didn't have any trouble with 'em. Anyway, they didn't ask about the kid . . . they asked about you."

"What about me?"

"If she knew where you were."

"And she didn't."

"That's right. Seems that Logan was about half mad at Hoyt for even botherin' her." Buck sank down upon a sack of barley, watching Jack shave. "Do you know why Hoyt took Logan there?"

"No, how would I know?"

Buck made a face. "I expect you wouldn't at that," he said. "Like I told you, Hoyt's no fool. He knows the girl's in love with you."

Jack turned and looked down. "She didn't tell you that, Buck."

"Nope. She didn't have to. Neither did Hoyt

Farmer. I know 'em both better'n they know themselves."

While Jack was still staring at him, the old man's muddy eyes turned saturnine. "There's something else you got to know, too, boy. A gunman rode into town today lookin' for Josh Logan."

Jack continued to stare at the liveryman in silence.

"I never seen him before, but I know who he is. He's got that look to him . . . that killer look."

"All right. Who is he?"

"The Sundance Kid."

Jack started visibly. "Are you sure?"

"I'll bet a good horse on it. He's sort of wiry, dark-faced-lookin', packs two guns, and limps."

Jack turned back and sluiced his face off. The years rolled back. Jack Britton—the Sundance Kid. Arizona's fastest gun for hire. He straightened up and patted his face.

Buck gestured toward the food. "Eat, boy. Unless I'm way off course, you're goin' to need your guts full before this day's over."

Jack ate and thought. Finally he spoke. "I want you to do something, Buck. First, did the Kid see Logan?"

"No. Logan left before sunup to go back to rail's end."

"Good. You go hunt up the Sundance Kid and. . . ."

166

"Won't be hard to do. He's stayin' at the hotel."

"All right. Go get him and fetch him back here."

The liveryman's eyes drew out narrowly. "You crazy? You . . . without even a gun?"

"It wouldn't do me much good if I had one. Go on, get the Kid and bring him back here."

Buck got up but made no move to leave. He squinted upward. "Son, I been around a lot longer'n you have. If you got a notion of talkin' the Kid out of gunnin' you, forget it. His kind kill unarmed men just as quick as armed ones, and, once they hire out, they don't swap horses."

Jack inclined his head in agreement, then spoke. "You're right, Buck. And you're also wrong. The Sundance Kid never killed an unarmed man in his life."

Buck lingered a moment longer, turning something over in his mind, then left. Jack finished eating, made a cigarette, and sat down to wait. It wasn't a long wait. He heard the ring of Mexican spurs before Buck entered the granary followed by a man with a very faint limp. The newcomer was dressed in faded clothing, and, except for the well-cared-for guns he wore, one lashed to each leg, and his constant air of wariness, he appeared to be a down-on-his-luck cowboy.

At sight of him memories stirred in the big man. He came out of the shadows with a sardonic grin.

"Hello, Kid."

The gunman stood perfectly still, letting his eyes become accustomed to the gloom, then he made a slow smile.

"Hello, Jack."

His voice was husky and strong-sounding. He did not offer a hand but his teeth shone through parted lips.

"Heard you was in this place."

"Who sent for you, Kid?"

"Feller named Josh Logan. You're not goin' by that name, are you?"

"No."

The Kid nodded and continued to study the big man, his smile fading. Jack used both hands to hold his coat out.

"No gun, Kid. . . ."

Britton's eyes flicked down, then up again. "You ain't turned preacher have you?" he asked with some humor.

"No. Did Logan wire you?"

"Yeah. Couple days ago."

"He wants you to kill a man, Kid."

Sundance glanced briefly at old Buck, then leaned against the wall. "I figured that," he said. "You work for him?"

"No, I'm the man he wants you to kill."

For a second the Kid's face sagged, then he frowned. "You?"

"Yeah."

Jack told the gunman how he happened to come

168

to Herd. He explained about his saddle shop and his friendship for a crippled boy. He mentioned Rob's parents, his uncle, and the uncle's unquenched hatred that had been passed on to the boy.

The Kid listened with his head averted, making a cigarette. When Jack finished speaking, he lit up, exhaled, and cast a long look at the big man. Finally he said: "I come a long way, Jack." Smoke trickled upward past his face. "This here Logan's to pay me five hundred for calling some feller out." He mouthed the cigarette, its tip glowed red, then a cloud of smoke erupted and momentarily shrouded the dark features. "How long's it been since you used a gun?"

"Better'n three years."

"I could probably beat you then," the Kid said.

"Maybe. More'n likely it'd be a draw. Two down. A man slows but he doesn't forget."

"Yeah." The Kid swore softly. "Dammit, Jack, we been pardners. I don't want to shoot it out with you . . . especially for money." The dark-brooding eyes lifted. They were thoughtfully steady. "This Logan . . . is he really as ornery as you just made him out?"

Jack gestured toward Buck. "Ask him. Ask anyone around here. Even the sheriff."

Sundance made a crooked grin. "He ain't around. That's the first thing I ask in a town . . . where's the law." The grin atrophied; the thoughtful, steady-eyed look returned.

"If you haven't met Logan yet, then you haven't hired out to him," Jack said.

"That's right."

"I'll hire you. For five hundred you don't call me out."

The Kid crushed his cigarette before answering. "Five hundred cash?"

"Gold or silver, take your pick."

"What else I got to do, Jack?"

"Meet Logan and stay with him. He's out at his railroad camp today. You'll get him back to town some way, then you'll stand aside while I call him out."

"Sounds fair," Sundance commented. "Is he fast?"

"I don't know."

"You'd better find out," the gunman said dryly. "I want you alive so I can collect my five hundred, Jack. You just hired a rider."

Jack thrust his hand out. The Kid shook it, then the big man started forward. "I'll go get you the money," he said. Sundance didn't release his hand.

"I got a hunch from seein' you hidin' in this granary, that you'd better not go outside. Forget the money for now. Let's work this thing out first."

Buck ran a shirt sleeve across his forehead and relaxed. When he spoke, his voice was reedy. "I'll give you the money, Jack."

170

Sundance turned slowly and stared at the old man. He said nothing for a time, then he grinned again. "Forget it, pop. I was only horsin' around. I've known Jack Swift of Tularosa for a long time. I figure I made a hell of a good trade here . . . bein' hired not to go up against him. He was one of the fastest guns you ever saw, a few years back." The Kid's smile broadened. "An' fight! Why god dammit, you never saw a man could dog-fight like Jack. I've seen him start at the door an' clean out a saloon full of cowboys with his bare hands."

Jack interrupted. "Kid, let's do some planning. Josh Logan's no fool."

He got no further. Sundance faced around and made a gesture with his left hand. "Oh, to hell with this Logan. You want him here in town . . . I'll bring him."

"Alone if you can work it," Jack said. "He's the railroad superintendent. He's got a big track crew working for him."

The Kid shrugged. "Alone if I can . . . with his track layers if I can't. Don't worry about them. I'll be here, remember. Logan'll play fair or I'll thin out his crew." The Kid's indifferent look vanished. His eyes warmed with recollection. "Jack, you recollect that little redhead at Ma Tomla's down in Laredo? Well, damned if Tex Connelly didn't up an' marry her, an' they got a little spread east o' Tucumcari. And of Calabasas? Well, he's workin' for the Chiricahua Land and Cattle Company down along the border . . . not very far from here in fact. An' Red Ewart, you remember him?"

Jack nodded.

"Believe it or not he's a lawman. A real honest-to-god deputy marshal. He's married, too. Lives over at Wagon Mound."

The Kid's voice faded a moment, then resumed. "Wait'll I see 'em. They'll never believe Jack Swift of Tularosa is a saddle maker in a two-bit cowtown."

Buck shuffled his feet a moment, then started for the door. "Excuse me, gents," he murmured. "I got a livery barn to run."

The Kid turned. "Sure, pop. By the way . . . you got a big breedy blood bay geldin' here. He's mine. Give him a bait of grain an' a rub-down."

"Be glad to," the old man said, looking at Jack impassively. "You be careful."

After he left, the Sundance Kid went to a grain sack and sat down. His brow was furrowed in thought. Eventually he spoke. "Feller hears talk when he comes to a strange town, Jack. I asked around a little when I first rode in. Folks're sort of steamed up about this squabble 'tween Logan an' a boy. Seems a few of the older ones recollect things about Logan they're diggin' up now."

"Like what?" Jack asked.

The Kid shook his head. "It's hard to get anyone to open up to a stranger." He stood and touched the two guns. "These things don't help any. But there's an old gaffer who cleans up at the hotel. He told me Logan's got a reason for tryin' to grind that kid into the dirt."

"Is that all he said?"

The Kid shook his head and moved to the door. "No. He said Logan's got somethin' inside him that sticks him like a knife every time he looks at that kid. Something he did a long time ago, something that folks don't know about."

Jack thought of Rob's mother, of her preference for Rob's father over his brother. No, it wouldn't be that. People knew about that.

His eyes narrowed with concentration. "Something people don't know about?"

"Yeah."

"Like what, Kid?"

"Hell, I don't know, or I'd tell you."

"Couldn't you get it out of the old man?"

The Kid's mouth pulled down. "I ain't very good at throwin' down on old folks. Besides, that old geezer wouldn't tell me anyway. I know his breed. Ol' buffalo hunter. Tougher'n a boiled owl."

"Buffalo hunter? Is he bald-headed an' does he sniffle when he talks?"

"That's him. You know the old cuss?"

"No, I've seen him is all. But I know who he is. He was a pardner of the kid's grandfather. Hereabouts he's called Uncle Ned."

Sundance began twisting up a cigarette. "Then

173

the kid's grandfather probably knew about this thing, too."

Jack crossed to the Kid's side. "You go get Logan and I'll find out what the old man's got on his mind." Jack pushed the door open farther. He gave Sundance a slight shove. "Go on."

"All right. But if I can't bring Logan back this afternoon, don't get upset. I'll have him here some time tomorrow. You just be patient an' keep your eyes skinned for us."

After Sundance left, Jack thought of his last remark. It didn't sound like the Sundance Kid, to him. In times past, when the Kid went after something, he got it. Still, it seemed a minor thing. He shrugged it off, went to the granary door, and peered out. Up near the roadside entrance Buck was talking to someone. He waited until the taller man turned, then recognized Deputy Will Spencer. Whatever was being said seemed to engross the deputy; he was standing with his head down and fisted hands pushed deep into his pockets.

Jack waited patiently until Spencer left, walking southward, then watched Buck hurry toward the rear of the barn.

As soon as he passed the granary door, the old man's words came tumbling. "You got to get out an' quick. Will didn't find any camp in the hills last night, but he found someone who saw you ride into town . . . one of Logan's spies. He just asked me to join a house-to-house search for you."

Jack stiffened. "Hell," he said. "They'll find Rob."

But Buck shook his head. "I'll take care of that. I got an idea. . . ."

"Not back here in the loft," Jack interrupted to say. "Logan's had this place watched since the trouble first started."

Buck looked mysterious. "Not here, either," he said. "Now you get." He turned away. "I'll saddle a horse and tie it out in the alley."

Jack caught the old man's arm. "First things first, Buck. There's an old feller at the hotel who told Sundance that Logan's got some special secret, something to do with his hatred of Rob."

"Never mind that," Buck said irritably, pulling away. "We'll worry about that later."

Jack did not relinquish his grip. "Listen . . . calm down, will you? I wouldn't get a hundred feet down that alley in broad daylight, afoot or on horseback. I've already had one run-in with Logan's men out there."

He could feel the old man's muscles turn slack under his hand. "But you can't stay here," Buck insisted. "Spencer'll go through this place with a fine-toothed comb."

"Go hitch up the hayrack," Jack said. "Throw some hay onto it and drive it down here and out into the alley. I'll get on and burrow into the hay."

"Hell," Buck protested. "I can't drive you all the way to the glass rock an' leave you there afoot, boy."

"You won't take me there," Jack said, giving the old man a push. "Get the rack and, when I get aboard, I'll tell you where to take me that Logan won't find me and Spencer won't think to look."

Buck went after the wagon and team, but he was badly worried. He had his day man pitch some hay onto the wagon, then drove it down through the barn after sending the hostler to the emporium for a ball of harness thread. A ruse.

Jack moved swiftly when the rack went by. He glimpsed Buck's white face only briefly, then was in the hay. Buck wheeled the team wide and swung southward down the alley. Jack burrowed up under the high seat and spoke crisply.

"Go around to the alley across the road," he said. "Like you're going to Southards' . . . only you aren't."

The liveryman obeyed, puzzled but hopeful. When he was abreast of a sagging old fence that enclosed the yard of the railroad company's Herd office, Jack spoke again.

"Just keep going. I'll leave you here."

Buck looked startled. "Logan's office?" He gasped incredulously.

But Jack was off the rack and moving through the broken gate.

Gaining entrance to the railroad superintendent's office was no problem. There were two rear windows; neither was locked although both were closed. Inside, the office was redolent of stale tobacco smoke and man sweat. It was poorly lighted, too, but this was in the big man's favor. Through a flimsy partition he could hear voices of people in the hotel lobby next door. He moved carefully around the room, noting the piles of reports and maps strewn everywhere. At a large, battered desk he sat down, studying the office, then he very deliberately took out a pocket knife and worked the lock to Logan's desk drawers loose. For half an hour he squinted at more progress reports in the gloom, and read copies of Logan's reports to the Kansas City headquarters of the railroad. These reports, stretching over a number of years, gave him a clear and composite picture of his enemy's steady rise to power, but they gave him no clue to the man's real character, nor had he expected them to. Then, in the act of replacing the papers, his hand inadvertently came in contact with something coldly metallic stuck to the underside of the drawer's inner fastness. He pulled the drawer fully out, got down on his knees, and looked up. The cold object was a tiny key that was held to the woodwork by a strip of gummed paper. He removed it, put the papers back into the drawer, and closed it, then went over by a rear window and examined his find.

The key was too small for Logan's desk, that was obvious. Nor was it large enough to fit the locks on the wooden filing cabinets. Then what, exactly, did it fit? It must be something in the office or Logan wouldn't have kept it there. He turned around and looked more sharply at the room. Whatever it fit, Logan clearly did not want it found; if he had hidden the key, he would also have hidden whatever it belonged to.

Excitement came; his heart thudded loudly. He started at the south wall and examined each piece of furniture, each drawer, each cabinet with minute care—and he found nothing.

He then returned to the desk, sat down, and tried to imagine where a man of Logan's temperament would hide something. Again he met with no success. Actually, beyond knowing that Logan was a vindictive and unscrupulous man, he knew nothing about his personality.

For a long time he sat there visualizing each piece of furniture, swiveled Logan's chair around, and stared at the walls.

Still nothing. There was no indication of a secret hiding place; each wall was of full-length planking. He got up suddenly and took three large steps forward—then stopped. A slightly metallic ring had come. He went back to the desk, reached down, and pushed Logan's chair far back, then let it snap forward. The sound came again. He spun the chair around, shook it, then went to work with his pocket knife, removing the back of the chair.

There was a small, dented tin box in among the chair back's wadding. He removed it with mounting excitement, went to a rear window, and inserted the key. It turned easily, the lid opened, and lying exposed to Jack's sight were a number of carefully folded papers, yellow with age and brittle to the touch.

He put the box on the desk, went to both front and rear windows for a careful study of the alleyway as well as of the main thoroughfare out front, then, reassured, returned to the desk and the chore of examining his find.

The first paper was a cancelled mortgage on some residential property in Herd, apparently Logan's home. There was a grant deed pinned to the mortgage and both were dated nearly twenty years earlier.

The second paper appeared to be someone's last will and testament. It was written in a very elaborate Spenserian script complete with shadings and flourishes. He laid it to one side and examined the third paper. This was a birth certificate. While holding it aloft with one hand, Jack rifled through the remaining papers, found them to be cancelled records of monetary loans to Joshua Logan, and left them in the box. Then, before attempting to read the papers he had kept out, Jack re-locked the little box, placed it carefully back in the chair's wadding, and screwed the backing into place again.

X

Briefly, as Jack sat at Joshua Logan's desk in the utter solitude of the gloomy office, a dazzling burst of hard yellow sunlight shot over distant mountains, fell into valleys, and spread with incredible speed over the desert floor to flood Herd with hot light. A wind-shaped wafting of gray clouds moved off and for a while Logan's office was brightened by this afternoon brilliance. Then, as swiftly and as unexpectedly as it had come, the yellow glare dissipated and the shadows came back. Jack made a cigarette, lit it, and spread the crisp paper with its Spenserian script before him on the desk top. In a clear but very archaic style, the will stated that the estate of Isaiah Logan, father of Jason and Joshua Logan, consisting of six thousand federal dollars, a wearisome list of personal items, and a four thousand acre ranch, was to be divided equally between Jason and Joshua. Reading further, Jack's eyes came to a codicil that caught his attention. Long-dead Isaiah Logan's bitterness showed through the precise wording—Joshua was to share in his father's estate only providing he made full and adequate provision for the rearing and educating of an illegitimate son.

Jack re-read the paragraph. The cigarette between his lips grew cold. He leaned back in

Logan's chair, picked up the birth certificate with cold fingers, and unfolded it. It listed a boy-child's weight, size, color hair, eyes, and—all that was omitted was that the child's eyes were of the deepest blue.

Jack put the certificate down, re-lit his cigarette, and stared at the father's name—Joshua Logan, not Jason Logan. Rob was Joshua's son, not the son of the man who had been killed in a flash flood—not the son of the man he thought was his father.

The still, hushed office seemed to turn cold.

Jack picked up the stage schedule. It was for the run between Herd and Bartlesville, Arizona Territory, and was dated ten years earlier. A heavy hand had encircled a date of departure from Herd and the time of arrival at Bartlesville, in blue crayon pencil. Pinned to the schedule was a cryptic message on faded yellow paper, the type of paper used by railroad telegraphers.

To: Section Foreman—Herd, A.T.
Warning Stop Bridge And Upper Dam Muerto Cañon Washed Out Stop You Have Two Hours Grace Stop Advise Evacuating Area Immediately Stop Chicago Notified.
Signed Belmont
Northfield A.T.

Written beneath this message on the same paper and in the same heavy blue-crayoned hand was a note to a stage company official stating that the railroad office at Herd had received word of possible danger that the Muerto Dam might wash out. It did not say that the dam had already washed out!

Josh Logan, knowing death was certain for anyone venturing into Muerto Cañon after the dam had burst, had deliberately permitted the stage company to send a coach into the cañon— driven by his own brother.

A stunned, icy sensation swept over the big man. He sat for a long time without moving, then very carefully refolded the damning evidence of murder and worse, put it all into his coat pocket, and left the desk to stand by the window, looking out.

Early evening's shrouded haze was coming over the range, over Herd, over the faraway mountains, as though to soil this day, or perhaps end it and cover one man's knowledge of another man's terrible iniquity.

A thought crossed his mind and he drew up, studying the roadway. There was no traffic at this quietly gray supper hour and that meant only one thing—Sundance had been unable to find Logan, or had not been able to bring him back to town. This, the big man thought, was unusual. Sundance always got what he went after.

He made another cigarette, not because he wanted it but rather to occupy his hands. When it

182

was fragrantly lit and the shadows were deepening, he lingered at the window waiting, but finally, certain that Logan was not coming, he left the office the same way he had entered it, through an unlocked rear window, and found the lowering darkness of night an ally while he went around behind Buck's barn.

There was a little riffle of chilly wind blowing up the valley. It swayed lanterns and moaned along the backsides of buildings. It also put a cold scent of hastening winter into the night. Another thing this ragged wind did was reveal a man standing south of Buck's place, stamping his feet and swinging his arms to keep warm. Beside him, leaning against a shed, was a shotgun.

Jack watched the coated figure, obviously one of Logan's spies. The man stamped with sufficient vigor to indicate that he resented his job, and thought it senseless. The big man moved across the alley among the far shacks, westerly, then completed a circle that brought him up beside the shed that shielded Logan's man. He inched along it, shot a careful look around a corner, and saw the shotgun less than three feet from him. He drew in a big breath, stepped out into plain sight, grabbed the shotgun, and flung it backward into the night. As the railroader was turning, attracted by the sound of his gun striking the ground, Jack pivoted his weight, dropped one shoulder behind the blow, and struck. Logan's man went over backward with an abrupt look of astonishment frozen on his face.

Jack used the sentinel's belt and scarf to bind and gag him. Then he rolled the man into the lee darkness of the shed and left him there.

From the darkness beyond the livery barn Jack could see old Buck part way up the runway, fidgeting with some harness. There was a top buggy between the old man and the alley entrance. This brought a thin smile to the big man's face; Buck never left a buggy out in the runway in his life. It was clearly a screen to hide the granary, and the alley entrance beyond, from the front entrance of the barn. Jack whistled, low, and moved into the swaying lantern light.

Buck turned, looked over his shoulder, then stabbed with a thumb toward the grain room door. The big man moved inside, angled right, and passed through the ajar granary door. Instantly, in that darkness, he was aware of a second presence.

"Jack . . . ?"

The voice was fluted and rising. He relaxed.

"Amy?"

She moved closer as he reached back and pushed the door farther open to admit light.

"Buck doesn't like the idea of me being here."

She was holding something out to him. It shone palely, like bone. He reached forth, felt it, and drew back his hand.

"Take it," she said, thrusting it at him. "It was my father's. It's loaded."

He was shaking his head when he answered. "I told you . . . it's against the law for me to carry a gun."

She pushed the steel against him. "You've a right to defend yourself. They mean to kill you, Jack."

He pushed the gun aside and reached for her. She came without resistance, put both hands against his chest, and tilted her head. He kissed her, and in the breathless moment when their lips touched she could feel the hot run of his temper and the deep hunger that was in him. Then he pushed her back.

"How's Rob?"

"Like a cricket," she said, a little unsteadily and thankful for the gloom. "Will Spencer searched the town a few hours back." Her teeth shone in a curved smile. "He didn't come to our house."

"Did he search here?"

The smile widened. "Not only the barn, but he even searched Buck's house."

Jack relaxed. "I guess it was wise of you two to move the boy."

She was straining to see into his face. "Buck told me about you sending that gunman after Logan."

He began to scowl. "I can't understand what's holding the Kid up."

"Perhaps Logan just wouldn't come. . . ."

Jack made a mirthless, short laugh. "He'd come,

185

all right. You don't know Jack Britton. When he goes after a man, he gets him."

She looked at the gun in her hand. "Do you suppose Logan has discovered that the Kid is working for you?"

Jack shook his head. "No. It's something else." He shrugged. "Well, the Kid said he might not be able to make it today."

"Tomorrow?"

"Yeah, tomorrow."

"Then please take this gun, Jack."

He regarded the gun thoughtfully, finally took it, and put it on a shelf. "Is your uncle around?" he asked, facing back toward her.

Amy was going to reply when voices came mutedly to them from beyond the granary door and up the runway near the top buggy. One voice was Buck's. The other, equally as unmistakable, belonged to Sheriff Hoyt Farmer. She touched his arm with one hand and put a finger to her lips. They moved stealthily forward and listened. Sheriff Farmer's drawl was clearly recognizable.

"Where is he, Buck?"

"Where is who?"

"Hell, let's not beat around the bush, Buck. You know damned well who I mean . . . your friend Jack Swift."

"Well, now," the old man retorted with exaggerated indifference, "what makes you think I'd know?"

"If you don't, nobody else does, Buck . . . unless maybe it's your pardner in this thing."

"What pardner?"

"My niece . . . Amy."

"Amy?" Buck replied scoffingly. "Why, that's the dangedest thing I ever heard, Hoyt."

"Is it?" the sheriff said quietly. "She's not home tonight, Buck. I figured she might be here talking to you."

"You can see that ain't so," the old man growled.

"Can I?"

"Sure." Buck was still speaking with emphatic conviction. "She ain't here . . . and furthermore, if you're after Swift, I got a hunch you've got a heap of ridin' to do."

"How so?"

"By now Swift an' the kid're a hundred miles from Herd and still goin'."

For a brief moment there was silence, then the sheriff said: "I kind of doubt that. I'll tell you why. On the stage up from Yuma I rode with a couple of strangers. Both of 'em was coming to Herd and both of 'em had come a long way in a big hurry to get here."

"What in hell has that got to do with Swift and the boy?" Buck demanded.

"If you'll give me a chance to finish," Hoyt Farmer said, "you'll maybe understand."

"Go ahead and finish then," Buck grumbled.

187

"One of the men was a border gun for the Chiricahua Land and Cattle Company. A young feller named Armstead."

"Armstead? What of it?"

"He used to have another name, Buck. The Calabasas Kid."

Jack and Amy could visualize Buck's look in the ensuing silence before Sheriff Farmer spoke again.

"The Calabasas Kid was an old friend of Jack Swift's. Then there was this other feller . . . a cowman, by golly, from over near Tucumcari, feller named Connelly. Tex Connelly. They told me they got another friend, too, who is on his way here. Feller named Red Ewart, a deputy U.S. marshal from down around Wagon Mound."

In a weak voice Buck said: "I don't understand."

"I do," Hoyt Farmer said. "Neither of those fellers knew I was the law hereabouts. I don't wear the badge in other counties. They told me a lot more'n I'd've told them. They're old friends of Jack Swift's. Someone sent 'em a telegram from here that he was in bad trouble."

"A telegram?"

"Yeah. As soon as I got back to town, I went to the telegraph office. Someone'd sent 'em word all right, but it wasn't Swift. The wire was signed with the initials S.K. Now then, you got any idea who S.K. is, Buck?"

The liveryman's answer was almost inaudible. "No, I don't think so."

"Then I'll tell you," the sheriff said, his voice quickening to a sharp, disapproving tone. "It stands for the Sundance Kid. He's in Herd, too . . . but of course you didn't know that . . . and he's also an teammate of Jack Swift's."

Buck said nothing. Jack and Amy heard the slow scrape of a match over a wagon tire, then smelled Hoyt Farmer's pipe.

"That's why I don't think Swift's left town, Buck. Because his old gunfighting friends are coming here from every direction to help him. Does that make sense, or doesn't it?"

Buck's answer was feeble. "I guess it does, Hoyt. Only. . . ."

"Yeah?"

"Well . . . god dammit . . . gunfighters mean bad trouble."

"That's no revelation," the sheriff said.

"Well, something ought to be done."

"Now you're getting wise, Buck. Something's got to be done, and fast, or there's going to be all hell bust loose. Now you tell me where Swift is so I can talk to him."

"You'll lock him up," Buck said faintly.

"Maybe . . . maybe not. If I do, I'll also lock Josh Logan up."

Buck's voice grew stronger. He had obviously made a decision. "You can't hold Logan, Hoyt. He'd be out in half an hour. But Logan'd frame Jack back into Yuma . . . and you'd uphold the law."

"That's my job."

" 'Fraid I don't set much store by your kind of law, Hoyt. Sorry . . . I don't know where Swift is."

"Buck," the sheriff said menacingly, "you old coot, I can also lock you up for aiding a fugitive."

"First you got to prove that's what I'm doin'."

There was an interval of silence, then the sound of Hoyt Farmer knocking his pipe against a wagon hub, and finally his soft drawl again.

"All right, Buck. Then carry a message for me. Tell Swift, if he buckles on a gun, even to defend himself, he's going back to Yuma. I didn't make that law, and I went to see the warden at Yuma Pen to see if he would overlook Swift carrying firearms just long enough to save himself."

"And . . . ?"

"The warden told me what I knew . . . that the law makes no exceptions."

Buck swore in towering disgust. "An' you got the guts to ask me to help you preserve that kind of law!"

Hoyt Farmer's voice grew more distant as he moved away from the top buggy, heading for the dark roadway beyond. "You tell him that, Buck. And you tell him I'm going to watch his friends like a hawk . . . after I get back from hunting up his hide-out in the hills tomorrow."

Buck did not appear at the granary door right away, and, when he finally did, he looked puzzled more than frightened. With only a glance at Amy he drew Jack back away from the door.

"That ain't like Hoyt at all," he told the big man. "He never rode out of town before when there was gunmen around. I don't understand it."

Amy spoke as she moved away from the door toward them. "I know my uncle very well. He will not compromise with his oath of office."

"Then why's he deliberately ridin' into them damned hills when he knows Deputy Spence searched 'em and found nothing?"

"Because he won't compromise with his principles, either."

"Huh?"

Amy was talking to Buck, but she was looking at Jack. "He believes a man has the right to defend himself. He also believes in upholding the law . . . if he was in Herd and trouble started. . . ."

Buck interrupted with a mild oath. "Hell! That's takin' the long way around, for me," he said.

Before he could continue, Jack touched his shoulder lightly. "Get me a horse, Buck. I got to go to Logan's camp . . . and fast."

"Why?" the old man demanded.

"Because, if Sundance got Connelly and Ewart here, that's where I think the trouble is going to bust out."

"No," Amy said quickly. "Not unless Josh Logan is there."

"But he is there," Jack said. Then, without

explaining, he gave Buck a slight push toward the door.

After the liveryman was gone, Amy looked into Jack's face briefly, and, when he made no move toward her, she went over by the door and stood there, looking out toward the alleyway. Jack stirred finally, roused from his thoughts by her obvious intention of departing.

"Amy?"

She turned as he came forward. "Yes?"

He was close to her, looking down. The full redness of her mouth was softly shadowed, as were her wide-open eyes. "Amy . . . I don't know exactly how to say it."

She did not help him. They stood motionlessly, gazing into each other's eyes, then he reached for her, drew her hard against him, and felt the full length of her body pressing into him. Her mouth was warm and yielding; she met pressure with pressure. When they broke away, at the sound of Buck leading a horse toward the alleyway entrance, she murmured: "You don't have to say it. I think I know. . . ."

XI

He rode northeasterly out of Herd with the cold making his breath white against the night. Near the scrub-oak knoll the sound of riders coming drove him to cover. He watched them pass, a bunched-up clutch of dark shapes, then resumed his way to the granite ledge overlooking Logan's railroad camp. He thought it likely, if Sundance had met Ewart, Connelly, and the Calabasas Kid, they would be in the neighborhood of the ledge. But when he arrived on the wind-swept plateau, there was no one there.

Below, much of the rubble had been cleared away and beyond the little work engine, where the gaping hole had been, was only a shallow depression. Logan had driven his men hard to repair the damage of the dynamiting.

There were more lanterns throughout the camp than there had been prior to the dynamiting, and, by looking closely, Jack could see armed men patrolling the roadbed, and beyond the camp where the dynamite cache was.

It was comforting to know that Logan had been hurt. It also consoled him to see that the railroad superintendent had put his camp on a military footing; the necessity for armed guards meant Logan would have fewer men available for posses.

But of Josh Logan or the men Sundance had summoned, there was no sign.

Jack rode down off the ledge, circled the camp, and rode toward the corrals. He found dozens of animals, mostly mules, and mounds of harness, but he found nothing to indicate that his old friends or Josh Logan were at rail's end. As he rode away, bound for Herd, he thought it possible that the men he had passed near the oak knoll might have been his friends and Josh Logan. In fact, he could think of no alternative for the disappearance of the men he sought.

The ride back toward town was slow. He had plenty of time for thought. The prospect of a showdown with Logan occupied his mind only briefly. Then he thought of Logan's bitter secret.

What kind of a woman had Rob's mother been? What kind of a man had Jason Logan been? What powerful motives had driven him to marry Rob's mother and raise his brother's illegitimate son? What corroding bitterness had Jason Logan known when he had seen the wild plunge of storm-churned water bringing inescapable death to him? Had he known his own brother had deliberately sent him into that cañon to die?

From his reflections emerged a vision of Logan's ruthless features. He recalled most of what the superintendent had told him the only time they had talked. From those words and what he had subsequently discovered about Logan, he considered the matter of killing him something very close to a duty.

It was this consuming determination that temporarily robbed him of his wariness. He did not underestimate his enemy; he simply did not consider Logan's wiliness until, within sight of the lights of Herd, two separate bands of riders suddenly charged toward him from either side of the road. As fate would have it, he heard the rocketing thunder of their approach before they were close enough to fire. It required only a moment for him to understand that Logan had stationed these men in ambush for him. And in that moment he drove home the spurs and leaped ahead in a belly-down run.

The pursuit closed in for a hundred yards, then, as his mount strained ahead, the railroaders dropped back slightly. What piqued Jack was the fact that, although he could see the wicked black reflection of naked guns, the ambushers did not fire at him. The reason for this came to him while he was less than a hundred yards from Herd's north entrance. Up ahead, standing ready on the outskirts of town, were four armed men. He wasn't certain but he thought one of them resembled Logan.

He reined hard around. The livery horse bent to the right in a dirt-spewing curve and headed straight for the alley behind Buck's barn. Someone, among the men standing in the roadway, shot at him. The bullet was wide and high. A man's roaring shout shivered the night air and other men, calling sharply, reined frantically toward the alley into which Jack had disappeared.

Jack passed the rear entrance to the livery barn with only an inward glance. Up near the center of the stable Buck's night hawk was standing, wide-legged, in a listening stance, then he began to turn. But the big man was past by then, bound for the south end of Herd. He popped out of the alley like the seed from a grape, shot down through the shanty section of town, scattering dogs right and left, then burst out upon the flat plain that ran out to Herd Creek. He did not slacken speed until the town lay well behind, then he cut westerly toward the bend of the creek, slowed his mount, and rode the last two hundred yards in a walk.

At the creek he dismounted, drank, permitted his horse only a few swallows, moved deeper into the willows, and waited. It was not a long wait; the sharp ring of a shod hoof striking stone urged him to remount and work his way carefully through the willows along the creekbank.

A lowering moon came from behind big-bellied clouds and shone with silver brilliance. Jack moved through the filigreed shadows like a wraith. The ground was soft, spongy, and resilient. It took impressions well but it also muffled the sound of his passing. Once, a mile upstream, he halted in a cottonwood clump to watch the back trail. Three easy-moving riders loomed out of the darkness. One was smoking a cigarette; with each inhalation its red end glowed cherry-like.

The strangers came on slowly, riding somewhat apart, and obviously tracking him through the mud. He thought at first they might be Sundance and his friends, but, when they got closer, he saw that their mounts were large, unwieldy combination animals, the kind no horseman would ride except as a last resort.

Jack left the creek and rode steadily down the night, far enough out in the curling dead grass to eliminate tracks. He rode for an hour, thinking he had lost the pursuit, when suddenly he heard a man hoot loud and call out: "Here! Here in the grass! Them's his tracks sure as' shootin'."

Jack swung directly away from the creek after that, and rode due north in a choppy lope. He sought for a hiding place and found none big enough for a man and a horse. The countryside ahead was pure desert, flat and rockless. Once, swinging slightly to the west, he was sure he heard other horsemen somewhere between Herd and the men who were trailing him. This prompted caution again. He booted the livery horse into a steady long lope and headed for the oak knoll, several miles distant, the only place he could think of where a solitary unarmed man might successfully elude Logan's bloodhounds.

Behind him the pursuit fanned out. Up ahead, in the quiet of the night, Jack could hear them coming. He attempted a ruse, swung west and rode steadily in that direction until it seemed he must be beyond the foremost pursuer, then reversed himself, rode south as far as a land swell topped by spidery paloverdes, dark against the waning night, and stopped to listen and look.

He did not see the rider appear through the darkness behind him, stop suddenly, study the big man's back, then fade out into the night, still behind him.

For a time his horse could rest; there was no immediate peril. Then, some minutes later, he heard the jangle of rein chains followed by a man's cough. He turned abruptly and eased down off the land swell, riding away from the gray-dawning saw-toothed mountains. He considered returning to Herd but gave up the notion at once. Logan knew about Buck's barn; he had men watching for him elsewhere, he was sure, and the only other refuge would be Amy's house. That was clearly out of the question. Thus far Amy was free of more than passing suspicion. So long as Rob was hidden there, he must do nothing to direct Logan's suspicion toward the Southards.

He thought of going to the glass-rock flat. But it was too far. If he was going to meet Logan, he would have to stay closer to Herd. Then he heard a shot. In its echoing stillness came two more, then a crashing volley of shots. He reined up sharply, probing the night behind him. The firing ended as abruptly as it had erupted. He was still trying to place the sounds when a single explosion came. It was east of him and the hum of the bullet drove him low over the saddle horn cap. He spun away and spurred toward an eroded sandstorm spire nearby, on his left. Behind him, a man's yell, raised in triumph, quivered in the nocturnal hush, then he heard a running horse sweeping down on him.

He got to the spire with moments to spare, left his horse in a leap, and flattened against the ground behind the crumbling upthrust. The strange rider came up fast, cut out around the spire, and went careening away into the night. Jack watched him go, carbine held high and ready. Unexpectedly a shot broke into the running horse's echo. Jack heard the animal snort, break his lead, then go trotting off. He could barely make out the riderless animal. Someone was behind him. Whoever it was, he had shot the man who had been after him. He assumed both the men were railroaders and that the mounted man had been shot in error. He had no reason to believe otherwise until a crouched figure moved into sight from the direction the mounted man had taken. Then he recognized the scarcely discernible limp of the Sundance Kid. For a moment, held silent by doubt and puzzlement, he watched the Kid approach, then he called out.

"Sundance!"

The Kid halted in mid-stride, quirked a hard look toward the sandstone spire, then came on, gun cocked and riding low in his hand. When he saw Jack, he stared briefly, nodded, then knelt at his side.

"One down, nine to go," the Kid said.

"Nine?"

The Kid nodded and lowered his gun. "Yeah, that's how many Logan took to town from rail's end with him. That one I got . . . that was the one called Cavin. He rode into me. The others are all around us."

"Where are Red and Tex and Calabasas?"

Sundance looked around. "You know, huh?"

"I know. The sheriff was talking about a couple of strangers he met on the stage up from Yuma. It wasn't hard to figure it out, Kid . . . only you shouldn't have brought them in."

Sundance looked reprovingly at Jack. "No?" he said. "Any time I go up against a whole god-damned army, you can bet your boots I'm not going alone."

"But Red's a lawman now. You put him in a hell of a spot."

"Naw," Sundance dissented. "Red's Red. He likes a good fight . . . badge or no badge. Anyway, he's got some influence around the territory, and with a plug hat like Logan we'll need a little of that."

The Kid peeked around the sandstone spire and mused aloud. "Wonder where the other ones are. We met 'em comin' up behind you and scattered 'em with a dose of lead . . . but I'm bettin' they didn't run far."

"They probably left the country," Jack said.

"They thought they were chasing an unarmed man and suddenly you came up shooting."

Sundance made a crooked grin. "It sure scattered 'em." He chuckled. "They broke up like a covey of quail." He looked over his shoulder. "Red an' Tex an' Calabasas ought to be comin' up about now. They were spread out on both sides of me when that idiot Cavin liked to rode over the top of me."

Jack touched his arm. "What happened between you and Logan?"

Sundance snorted. "I never got close, boy. Somethin' you didn't know . . . that telegrapher in Herd works for Logan. As soon as I wired for the others, he sent Logan word of it. I was lucky to get out of Logan's camp with a whole hide." Sundance shrugged. "But that's all right," he growled. "I like it better this way. Everybody knows who their enemies are. It makes a lot cleaner fight this way." He cursed, shot another look over his shoulder, and concluded with: "Now what'n hell's holding up Red and Tex an' that strung-out beanpole of a Calabasas?"

But Jack's thoughts were on Logan. He said: "When I was darn' near ambushed in town, where were you?"

"Comin' into town from the east. The boys an' I'd just made a sashay up near rail's end. We figured we might catch Logan alone. But evidently he'd already lit out for town."

"He was standing in the roadway when his boys jumped me," Jack explained. "I doubt if he came out here with 'em, though."

"Naw, not him. He ain't the kind," Sundance replied. "He does the plannin', not the fightin'."

"In that case I think I'll head for town."

Sundance looked surprised. "You runnin' out?" he demanded.

"No," Jack said, getting to his feet. "But my fight's with Logan, not his railroaders."

Sundance was going to speak when a bullet hit the spire above Jack and showered them both with dust. As Jack dropped down with an oath, the Kid smiled. "Guess you got a fight with the railroaders, after all. Leastways, anybody that shoots at me I don't call a friend." He drew his spare pistol and held it out. "Here, you can be a Holy Joe in town, but out here I'd recommend you do a little shootin'."

Jack hesitated, looking at the blue-black six-shooter in Sundance's hand. When he made no move to take it, the Kid tossed it into his lap.

"You go ahead be law-abidin'. Me, I'd rather be a pallbearer than a corpse."

A gun exploded east of the spire. Both the crouching men heard lead slap into sandstone. Sundance cursed, looked backward again, and swore at the others who had not yet made their appearance.

A flurry of rifle shots off to Jack's right made

him flatten against the ground. "They're flanking us," he said. Sundance was shucking spent casings and reloading his handgun. He made no reply.

A second shot struck the front of the spire, but this time the gunman was closer. Sundance went flat, shook off powder-fine dust, and growled: "I'm going to get that clodhopper."

Jack felt the steel of Sundance's gun near his fingers. He looked at the gun, watched his fingers close around it, lift, and cock it. Breath rattled past his parted lips. He shot a glance at the Kid. Sundance was watching him. He made his crooked little grin and began inching over the ground, around the base of the spire. Jack started to follow him, then a tinkle of spurs made him whirl. A cadaverous, tall shape materialized out of the night. It was holding a cocked carbine with both hands. Jack touched Sundance, who turned slowly, gun swinging. Jack heard the long sweep of breath going into the Kid's lungs.

"Calabasas!"

The lanky figure moved up and crouched. From a sunken pair of gray eyes a glimpse of hard humor looked toward Jack. The Calabasas Kid's teeth shone.

"Jack Swift! Who'd ever expect we'd meet here tonight? What a cussed coincidence."

Jack couldn't repress a grin. With equal hard irony he replied: "Yes, sir, sure is a small world, isn't it? You just happening by like this."

Sundance interrupted. "When you two are through makin' eyes at each other, there's a peckerwood out front of this god-damned rock that's got our range. Calabasas, you go around to the right. I'll go around to the left. And, Jack, you stay here."

Calabasas was crawling away when a stentorian bellow froze him in his tracks. Jack, too, raised up in surprise. He alone of the men behind the spire recognized that voice. It belonged to Deputy Sheriff Will Spencer.

"Hey! Put down those guns out there. This is the law!"

From behind Jack, out in the night a nasal voice drawled: "You don't say. Well, now, I'm sure obliged we got the law on our side, Mister Deputy. But I'd like it a heap better if I could see your badge. Somehow you sort of smell like railroad ties to me."

Jack was going to call out that he knew it was the law, when Spencer's angry voice came again. Jack placed Will's position that time. He was north of the spire somewhere, hidden in the darkness.

"Listen, I'm Deputy Will Spencer from Herd. I order you railroaders to put down your guns and stop this fighting. That goes for you other fellers, too. I know who you are an' I'm ordering you to stop shooting!"

The same nasal voice replied: "Well, now,

Mister Lawman, if you aren't on our side, an' if you won't be on the side of the railroaders, why then, just you get up on one of those little hills yonder and find yourself a nice seat, and watch the god-damnedest fight you ever saw!"

Sundance laughed. "That's Tex," he said.

Before Deputy Spencer spoke again, Jack raised his voice.

"Tex, that is the law. I know the voice."

From the darkness Connelly cried out: "That you, Jack? Sure good to hear you again, pardner."

"Tex, listen to me. . . ."

"Now Jack," the nasal voice said reprovingly. "You know damned well we can't lay our guns down. Why, that Logan feller'd have us crucified by dawn if we went back to Herd with your deputy friend. We can't hold still for that, boy."

Sundance and Calabasas crawled back beside Jack. They both concurred with Tex Connelly.

For a while there was silence. The light in the east was widening. Finally Sundance stood up and dusted his britches off. He studied Jack's face in the shadows. "Come on, Calabasas. Let's get out of here before sunup catches us."

The thin man got to his feet. So did Jack. "Wait," he said to both gunmen.

Calabasas smiled understandingly. "Hell of a thing when a feller's got principles, Jack. You always was like that. It makes life sort of complicated. Now I'm not sayin' I don't have

'em, but they don't include sittin' in a jail."
Calabasas's tawny eyes fixed themselves on
Jack's face. "You comin' with us or goin' with the
deputy?"

Before Jack could answer, Sundance spoke to
him.

"Listen, old son . . . if you let them put you in
their jail, Logan'll give you the big six. He'll get
to you through a window or a door, but he'll get to
you. You'd best come with us."

Jack nodded. "All right. But I've got something
I want the sheriff to have."

Sundance scratched his cheek, then shrugged.
"All right, call your deputy up here. We'll get
around the spire. If he throws down on you, we'll
disarm him." The Kid tilted his head. "But let's
not waste any more time. It'll be light directly."

Jack called out, facing north. "Will . . . ?"

"Yeah."

"Come on over here by this sandstone needle."

The deputy moved forward without another
word. When he was close enough to see Jack, he
reined up, looked around, then swung down, and
led his horse the last hundred feet. His expression
was sardonic.

"Like usin' a tied chicken to bait up a coyote,"
he said.

Jack had put Sundance's gun inside his
waistband under his coat. Will saw the bulge,
stared, but said nothing about it. In fact, he didn't

speak at all until Jack had taken some folded papers from his pocket and was holding them out. "What's that?"

Jack ignored the question. "I want you to give these to Hoyt Farmer. Don't show them to another living soul and don't read them yourself."

Spencer's face lifted. "No? Mind tellin' me somethin'? Where did you get 'em, Jack?"

"From Logan's office in town."

The left-handed deputy did not look surprised. He put out a hand, took the papers, and pocketed them. "All right. Hoyt'll get 'em and I won't look at 'em . . . unless Hoyt asks me to." He buttoned the flap over his pocket. "Now then . . . you comin' back to town with me?"

"Afraid not, Will."

"No," the deputy replied dryly, looking at the sandstone spire. "I didn't figure you were." He went up to his horse, mounted, and looked straight down at Jack. "I know about your friends. So does Hoyt and so does Logan. Jack, you haven't got a legal leg to stand on. You got no right to the kid. You're a fugitive from the law . . . an' I think you're packin' a gun. Can I give you a little advice?"

"Sure, Will."

"Ride on. While you're free . . . saddle up an' leave the country."

"I can't."

"Why not?"

"I told Rob a man didn't run from trouble, Will. I told him that the night I brought him back from the mountains. He came because he believed in me. How would it look if I ran now?"

Spencer lifted his reins, nodded in silence, and rode back the way he had come.

XII

Five hard-riding horsemen clattered toward the brightening horizon in a tight group. The man beside Jack wore a broad smile.

"Sure good to see you again," he was saying. "Takes a feller back a few years to be ridin' like this."

A thick-shouldered man with a fierce longhorn mustache interrupted by throwing up an arm and pointing. "There go Logan's railroaders." He smiled wolfishly. "I'll bet they hit their boss up for more money. Thought they were chasin' an unarmed man . . . and run up against us."

The man beside Jack chuckled. "When that deputy come up, they run for home like a bunch of kids caught stealin' from the cookie jar." He looked down at the bulge under Jack's coat. "You use that thing, boy?"

Sundance answered for Jack. "Naw, he didn't use it. But I got a feelin' he might. How about it, Jack?"

"I'll use it, but not if we keep riding this direction. Logan's back in Herd."

Red Ewart slowed his horse, looped the reins, and went to work on a cigarette. From behind the wicked curl of his big mustache he said: "Jack, what do you know about Logan that'd be a federal offence?"

"Nothing, Red. Not a blessed thing."

Connelly, still grinning, joined the conversation. "Leave him handle it his way, Red. He knows what he's doing."

"Sure," Ewart replied, lighting up. "But I'm a lawman, too, remember. I hadn't ought to be a party to a killing unless it's legal-like."

Calabasas laughed. "We'll make it legal-like, won't we, Sundance?"

"Sure, legal as all get out. Listen, you hop toads, I got an idea. That Herd lawman knows two of us. We came here on the Yuma stage with him. But there's one of us he doesn't know."

"Me," the deputy marshal said. "I know what you're thinking, Sundance. You're figuring I could go into Herd."

Sundance nodded. "That's right. The law knows me, it knows Tex and Calabasas an' Jack. It doesn't know you . . . at least not your face."

"All right. What about it?"

"You get Logan to take a ride with you . . . and bring him to us."

"He couldn't do it," Jack interposed. "You tried it and failed. By now Logan'll be suspicious of all strangers."

Sundance was undaunted. "All right then, he can still hang around town and watch for Logan. When he rides out, Red can trail him . . . signal his direction . . . and we can intercept him. That'd work just as well."

They rode a short distance, turning this over in their minds. Meanwhile, the sun popped up over a distant black snag of mountain and poured yellow light down on the desert. Jack halted and looked over the desert to get his bearings. They were several miles northeast of Logan's railroad camp, farther out on the desert than he'd ever been before. Nearby was a clump of ragged cottonwoods. At their base was the only greenery in sight. He dismounted and walked toward the trees, leading his horse. The others followed his example. When they were all in the shade, horses grazing, Red Ewart sprawled under a tree, pushed his hat back, and looked at the others.

"It might work," he said. "The worst that could happen would be that Sheriff Farmer'd catch me . . . and I've got a bigger badge than his. He couldn't hold me."

Jack was torn between his desire to meet Logan, and his fear that Ewart might be walking into more trouble than Jack had any right to ask him to risk. He sank down on the grass, thinking.

It was Sundance, supported by the Calabasas Kid, who argued heatedly in favor of the plan. Finally Tex Connelly sided with Sundance and

Calabasas. Because Ewart was willing, this left Jack alone in his opposition. Red got up, tugged his hat forward, and started for his horse.

"I'll signal with a pocket mirror," he said over his shoulder. "One flash . . . Logan's bound for the railroad camp. Two flashes . . . he's heading for Herd from the camp. Three flashes . . . he's riding south on the stage road. You got that?"

Jack nodded, watching the deputy marshal swing across his mount. "One more signal, Red. If Logan's alone . . . one long flash. If he's got his crew with him . . . two long ones."

Ewart nodded, cast a look at the others, then bobbed his head, spun his horse, and loped southwest across the burning land. Jack watched him go; he had misgivings. Sundance, watching him from beneath a tugged-down hat brim, said: "You worry too much, boy. Red's been around a long time. Nothing'll happen to him."

Jack lay back, saying nothing. The shade, the cool green earth under him, and the rhythmic grinding of jaws where the horses grazed worked a subtle magic. He was dozing off when, as though from a great distance, he heard Tex Connelly say: "Damn. I'm hungry enough to eat the stripes off a skunk."

It was close to sundown when a long shadow fell over him and a bony hand shook him by the shoulder. Jack opened his eyes with an effort. The Calabasas Kid grinned into his face.

"Hey, boy, you goin' to sleep till Doomsday? Tex's got three sage hens cookin' an' we got the signal from Red."

Jack got up stiffly. His back ached and his joints felt stiff. From over where a small fire glowed and the fragrance of roasting meat came, Sundance looked up with a dry smile.

"Didn't used to take you that long to come up out of dreamland," he said laconically.

Tex Connelly laughed and held out a twig with sizzling meat on it. "Here, drape your fangs around this, boy. It'll make you feel like culling wildcats while you're waitin' to tangle with Logan."

Jack took the meat, and the joshing, in silence. After he had eaten a little, he looked over where Calabasas was sprawling. "Well," he said. "What'd the signal say?"

Calabasas didn't answer; Sundance did. "It said Logan's headin' for town . . . with two long flashes."

"His crew," Jack mused.

Sundance wiped his fingers on the grass and flexed them. "Nothin' to worry about there, Jack. When the day comes us fellers can't handle a posse of railroaders, we ought to hire out as sheepherders."

"How long ago did Red signal?" Jack asked.

"Just before Calabasas woke you." Sundance looked at Connelly and Calabasas. "Well, you fellers goin' to keep fillin' your faces all night . . . or shall we hit the trail?"

Tex groaned and cast aside a glistening bone. "This is damnedest country I was ever in for goin' hungry. If I was home, now. . . ."

"Yeah," Calabasas said, getting to his feet. "If you was home that wife of your'n would have you dungin' out a hen roost or somethin'." He yawned and stretched. Then an idea came and his face brightened. "Tex, I know what's wrong with you . . . you got worms. Belly worms." He beamed at Jack and Sundance. "If you fellers'll hold him down, I'll make some worm medicine like we de-worm cattle with, and pour it down him."

Sundance got up with a laugh. Even Jack looked amused. Tex threw Calabasas a withering look and stood up. "One thing wrong with you," he said to the tall, thin gunman. "You got two brains in one head."

Calabasas sniffed suspiciously. "Two? Well, what's wrong with that? Two're better'n one."

"Depends," Connelly replied, heading for the horses. "Depends on their damned size. With you, now, one's the size of a pea an' the other's a little bit of a thing."

Calabasas swore and Sundance guffawed. They both followed Jack to the horses and swung up. Tex gestured with his right arm.

"Go on, Jack, this is your party. Lead the way."

Jack led out. Day was fast fading. Overhead,

wind-shaped clouds cast ribbon-like shadows over a steely sky. Ahead, miles of flat country lay across their vision, broken only by spiny vegetation, until Jack saw the oak knoll. He swung south, passed the road leading to Herd from rail's end, and pushed steadily through the dying day until a series of square blocks showed against the horizon.

As Herd drew closer, Sundance spoke. His eyes were squinted nearly closed and his face was set in stone. "Jack, this here Logan's got quite a mob if he's got 'em all with him. I figure maybe you an' Tex an' me had best stick close together."

"How about me?" Calabasas demanded.

"You watch that damned sheriff an' his deputy."

"If they're together, I will," Calabasas retorted. "If they ain't, I'll watch the deputy. I figure he's the aggressive type."

"Left-handed lawman," Tex snorted. "Never saw one in my life amounted to a damn."

"I think," Jack said, "Red'll be watchin' the law. If he is, Calabasas, you hunt the rest of us up."

Sundance urged his mount ahead, then reined up to study the town. When the others came up, he said: "Looks all right to me. Not too quiet . . . not too noisy."

Jack noted mentally that the town sounded about as it always sounded. Still, he had a queasy sensation in the pit of his stomach. When they were close enough to see people moving along the plank walks, Jack unbuttoned his coat. Sundance's second gun glinted evilly. When the others crowded up close, Jack said: "Now listen. This is my fight. I want Logan."

"Hell, he's yours," Tex Connelly chirped cheerfully. "All I want is something decent to eat." He shook out his reins.

"Couple things I'd like to know before we get into this thing," Sundance asked Jack. "First off . . . what becomes of the kid if you kill his uncle?"

"He'll be an orphan," Jack answered. "And I'll adopt him."

Three heads turned simultaneously. It was Calabasas who overcame his astonishment first. "You . . . adopt a kid?"

"What's wrong with that?" Jack demanded quickly.

"Nothin'. Nothin' at all . . . 'cept . . . well. . . ."

"Oh, hell," Tex growled at Calabasas. "We all grow up sometime. Can't spend your whole life ridin' around wavin' a gun off a fast horse . . . you simpleton."

"No," Calabasas said quickly, seeing the hard looks. "No, of course not. I . . . it just come on me sudden-like is all. No harm in it at all. In fact, I think. . . ."

"That's just it," Connelly grunted. "You don't think."

"The other question," Sundance queried. "What else you got against Logan, besides the way he's been treatin' the kid?"

Jack looked long at them. Each weathered face had hard lines; each pair of eyes had a depth of deceptive calm; each mouth was a straight line. He had lived with these men; he had drunk and fought and shared secrets with them.

"I'll tell you what else I've got against Logan. . . ."

He told them. They listened. When he was through talking, they looked toward the town and back to one another's faces again. It was Sundance who said: "Wouldn't be right for the kid to ever learn about that, would it?"

Everyone agreed that it would not.

Jack lifted his reins. "Come on, the more we talk the less I like sitting here."

They followed him as far as the east alleyway, which led down behind the saddle shop. But Jack didn't go that far south. He stopped at the hitch rack of the General Store, swung down, and tied up. Sundance, Connelly, and the Calabasas Kid followed his example. They moved away from the horses when Jack did. He went toward a dogtrot between two buildings and faded into its darkness, heading for the main thoroughfare beyond.

At the dogtrot's exit Jack stepped out onto the plank walk. South of him several doors was the railroad superintendent's office. A bright orange square of lamplight shone out into the roadway. Across the road were shuttered stores and the long run of the roadway. Buck's barn had both carriage lamps lit. Not far from the stable's entrance

Sheriff Farmer was in deep conversation with a man whose back was to Jack. Nearer, but also across the way, several men in flat-heeled boots were lounging under an overhang in a little group. There were four of them. Jack nudged Tex Connelly who was beside him.

"See those clod heads yonder by the barbershop, the ones with flat heels?"

"Yeah. They railroaders?"

Jack nodded. "Probably the same ones that tried to bushwhack me earlier."

"There were more than four, that time," Calabasas said, eyeing the lounging men. "Want me to sashay over there and . . . ?"

"Not yet," Jack said quickly, seeing Calabasas begin to edge toward the roadway. "Let's spot the others."

A livery rig whirled past, heading for Buck's barn. Behind it, jogging easily, rode two ranch hands. The man Sheriff Farmer had been talking to turned suddenly and walked swiftly across the roadway, heading for the hotel. The way he slammed his feet down indicated anger. Jack watched him, saw the broadcloth suit and the bowler hat—and wondered.

"There's three more," Sundance said suddenly. "Yonder, this side of the sheriff's office."

Jack looked. It was not hard to identify Logan's men. Their dress separated them from both cowmen and townsmen. Also, they stayed to themselves, did not offer to mingle with other people.

"That makes seven," Tex said. "Can't be a whole lot more . . . can there?"

Instead of answering, Jack simply shook his head. He was watching a fiercely mustached man who was smoking a cheroot in front of Cardoza's Saloon, half hidden by darkness. Beside him, also smoking a cigar and lounging comfortably, stood Deputy Will Spencer. Tex also recognized the mustached man.

"Hah, lookee yonder, boys. Red's runnin' with the herd. He's went an' bought the deputy a stogie." Connelly's chortle infected them all.

When Calabasas spoke next, he sounded pleased: "That leaves the sheriff all to me. I want to see the look on his puddin' face when he feels my single six in his kidneys." Calabasas shuffled his feet impatiently. "What say, Jack . . . all set?"

When Jack continued to study the pedestrians on both sides of the roadway without answering, Sundance spoke up.

"Come on, Jack, there's seven railroaders in sight. Calabasas can get the sheriff. Me 'n' Tex'll herd the railroaders together . . . an' that'll leave you an open field with Logan in his office."

The peculiar sensation Jack had felt beyond town returned. He felt unsure, apprehensive, but actually within his sight there was less to be concerned about than he'd seen under similar circumstances in years gone by. In those days he'd felt only the dark run of hot blood. Now, although he could not explain it even to himself, he felt uneasy.

Sundance nudged him. "Well . . . ?"

Jack pulled Sundance's extra gun from his waistband, checked its cylinder for loads, and put it back. In a voice gone cold and crisp, he said: "All right. I'll wait until I see you come up behind your men. Then I'll go down to Logan's office." He looked at the thin man. "Calabasas, that sheriff's a decent feller. . . ."

"Sure. I won't do him no harm."

They split up. The last one to move off was the Sundance Kid. He looked at Jack's shadowed face. "Boy, you take your time. If Logan's got more'n two of them railroaders in there with him . . . you wait for me. I'll be back. Remember that . . . more'n two."

Jack watched his friends cross the roadway through the darkness. He was so engrossed in their progress he did not notice that Red Ewart and Deputy Spencer were no longer standing under the overhang down by the saloon.

Sheriff Farmer had his head bent and his hands cupped around the match he was holding to his pipe when the thin, cadaverous shadow materialized behind him. Jack saw Farmer's head jerk up, his body stiffen.

He was so engrossed in this silent drama that he did not heed approaching footfalls until a man's voice said: "Easy, boy. It's me . . . Red."

Jack turned very slowly. Ewart was half smiling up at him.

"I thought you were with the deputy."

"No need now. He's gone to have a talk with Amy."

Jack blinked. "Amy Southard?"

"Yeah."

"You found out about her, Red?"

"Well, dammit, that's my trade, Jack. Nosin' around and figurin' things out. This here," Ewart said with a gesture around the town with one hand, "is kind of like a holiday for me. Sort of like attendin' a reunion and mixin' in a little work, too."

"What's he want with Amy?"

"To see that Rob's all right."

At Jack's blinking stare the deputy marshal's teeth flashed white from under the dark splendor of his mustache.

"They were bound to find out sooner or later, Jack."

"Does Logan know?"

Ewart wagged his head. "Not yet. Farmer and Spencer just found it out about an hour ago. Farmer went to see Missus Southard . . . she's his sister or something . . . and there was the kid, eatin' at the kitchen table."

"He will find out, though," Jack said, and started to move.

Ewart restrained him by one arm. "What difference does it make? Let him find out."

Jack pulled free. "He'll kill the kid, Red."

"Naw. Listen to me a second. Amy Southard got a lawyer from Raton. He got a writ of Mandamus against Logan."

"A what?"

"Writ of Mandamus. It means he's got to show cause why he wants you arrested."

"Well, for hell's sake . . . he can do that easy enough, Red."

Ewart nodded. "Sure he can . . . if he's around to do it."

"What d'you mean?"

"When that writ was served on him by Deputy Spencer, he come a-hightailing it back here to town with his crew."

"What of it?"

Ewart turned and pointed across the roadway where Hoyt Farmer was standing—with a thin shadow behind him. "Farmer's waitin' for Logan to come out of his office. He's goin' to call him."

"What! He can't do that. He's a law officer."

"Nope. He quit this afternoon." Ewart looked up again. "I guess you know why, Jack."

"Why?"

Ewart shrugged. "Don't ask me. All I can tell you is that he read some papers Will Spencer gave him. About an hour later he resigned, left the office, and has been waitin' around for Logan to show up ever since. He missed it when Logan come to town, boy, but he won't miss him this time if he has to stand there all night."

"Oh, no," Jack said. "Red, see that man behind Farmer there in the shadows, that's Calabasas. He's got the sheriff disarmed."

Ewart turned and squinted. After a time he said: "You mean you've already started your play?"

"Yes. Look yonder . . . where those four men're walking toward Buck's barn with that other feller behind 'em. . . ."

"Tex!"

"And there, yonder. Those others. . . ."

"Sundance!"

Ewart ran a nervous hand up along his mustache. His brow creased and his eyes narrowed. With deliberate slowness he turned back toward Jack. "We better stop it, boy. That writ an' the lawyer an' all. . . ."

Jack was shaking his head. "Too late to stop it, Red. You can come with me to Logan's office or. . . ."

XIII

Jack was moving away, starting southward along the plank walk when Red Ewart came out of his reverie. He hastened after the big man, caught his arm, and pulled him around.

"Listen to me a second, Jack," the deputy marshal said. "That writ of Mandamus will force Logan to give his reason for wanting you arrested."

"What of it?" Jack asked, puzzled.

"Dammit, he's after you 'cause you got his nephew."

"Yes."

"But he can't prove you got him, Jack. Until he has proof, he can't have you arrested. Do you see?"

Jack nodded. "Yeah, I see. I also see something you've overlooked. A couple of things in fact."

"Such as . . . ?"

"In the first place Logan's got enough railroaders working for him to swear me back into Yuma for carrying a gun. He's never seen me carry a gun any more'n he knows I have Rob, but that won't matter. He'll pay his men to swear in court under oath that I carried a gun. That's all it'd take to send me back."

Ewart said nothing. He was watching the big man's face closely and listening.

"The second thing is Hoyt Farmer. You know I sent him some papers. I can guess how you know. You wormed it out of Will Spencer. What you don't know is what was in those papers. Well, I'll tell you this much. Josh Logan deserves to die and those papers prove it. Hoyt Farmer knows that. Maybe he was a special friend of a man Josh

Logan killed. I don't know. I didn't suspect that when I sent him the papers or maybe I wouldn't have sent them to him. This much I do know and so do you. If Farmer kills Logan, it'll ruin him here in Herd. A lawman can't resign, shoot a man, then put his badge back on. Law enforcement is Farmer's life. I did this to him and I've got to prevent him from ruining his life by killing Logan myself."

Ewart frowned and shrugged. "All right, Jack, it's your game. I came along to see that you got a fair shake. I reckon you know more of the ins and outs than I do." Ewart looked southward along the plank walk where lamplight spilled onto the roadway from Logan's office. "You go ahead and do things your way. One thing though . . . Will Spencer is pretty upset over Farmer quitting as sheriff. He blames you for that, and he told me he knew you'd try and force a showdown with Logan." Ewart's eyes swung back to Jack's face again. "He's watching Logan's office, waiting for you to show up."

"From inside or outside?"

"Outside."

"Find him, Red, and don't let him interfere."

Ewart looked reluctant. Before he could speak again, a thin yell arose over the hushed town. A dark silhouette was running frantically from the direction of the livery barn. Both Jack and Red Ewart turned to watch. The running man's empty

224

hip holster flopped and his legs pumped like pistons. He was heading straight for Josh Logan's office.

From the doorless entrance to Buck's barn a second shadow appeared. There was a dark glint of steel showing. The second shadow called out.

"Hold it! Stop where you are!"

Jack recognized the voice; the second man was Sundance. He turned to see if the fleeing man would obey. He did not stop. Sundance fired, the fleeing man crumpled, dark dust arose around him, then he scrambled up and raced the remaining distance to Logan's office and slammed past the door.

Sundance's bitter profanity was loud in the quiet. He stood in the barn doorway, looking out for a moment, then he holstered his gun angrily, turned, and limped back into the shadows.

"That spoiled things," Ewart said in a detached tone. "Logan'll know now, for sure."

Jack felt bitter; he had wasted precious time. Without another glance at Red Ewart he started forward. The plank walk was empty. In fact, the entire town seemed empty. There was no one on either walkway and the road was devoid of traffic. A sickle moon glowed and thin light shone against the far mountains.

Jack was less than fifty feet from the railroad superintendent's door when the lights went out. He stopped, then moved quickly sideways to press against the building. Red Ewart was no longer in sight. Into the powerful stillness Sheriff Farmer's voice came, brittle-sounding and hollow.

"Logan!"

The silence ran on. No answer came from the office.

"Logan! This is Hoyt Farmer. I know how many railroaders you got in there with you . . . six. Listen to me, Logan . . . there are six men waiting out here for you to come out. Six . . . counting me. You think you got seven men outside here, too, but you haven't. That feller who escaped'll tell you where your other men are . . . in the livery barn unarmed and under guard. You got a pretty slim chance Logan, but no one'll shoot you if you walk out of there unarmed. You'd better do it . . . you and your men."

Jack could not see where Calabasas and Hoyt Farmer were standing. The west side of the road was in complete darkness except for pale lamplight coming from deep within Buck's barn.

He wondered if Calabasas had given the sheriff back his gun. Farmer had said there were six of them waiting for Logan. Jack knew of only five, including himself—Sundance, Ewart, Calabasas, and Tex Connelly. It didn't matter. He didn't intend to let Farmer kill Logan.

The sheriff's voice came again, as bitter-sounding as before: "Logan! You're covered front and rear. You've got to come out sometime. These fellers out here can wait longer'n you can. . . ."

Jack heard the muffled sound of voices in the office. Logan's men were arguing. He smiled thinly; railroaders weren't gunfighters. Then the superintendent answered Hoyt Farmer.

"What the hell d'you think you're doing, Sheriff? You're the law. Those men out there are gunmen . . . outlaws. Swift did ten thousand dollars' worth of damage to the railroad. He's a fugitive from the law. . . ."

"Logan, I resigned. I'm not sheriff any more."

There was an interval of deep silence. Jack could hear the raised voices in the office through the wall, but beyond, the full length of Herd, there was not a sound. Then Hoyt Farmer spoke again.

"Logan, you remember who my first deputy was? You remember whose wedding I was best man at? You recollect who the feller was who worked hardest to get the new stage line going?"

Jack understood. He knew Joshua Logan also understood. Hoyt Farmer was talking about Logan's dead brother, the man who had married a girl Logan had courted and wanted, the man who had raised Josh Logan's son as his own son. The sheriff's brittle voice went on.

"You ruined a lot of lives, Logan . . . now you're going to pay for every one of them. You better send those railroaders out of there. These men're going to smoke you out, starve you out, or burn you out."

Straining against the wall, Jack heard a violent argument break out in the office. He was listening with his head pressed close and neither saw nor heard the approach of a newcomer, until cold steel pressed against him.

"Give me that gun, Jack."

He turned very slowly. Will Spencer was standing there, white-faced, holding out his right hand.

Jack could hear his own heart sloshing erratically. "Will. . . ."

"The gun."

Jack took it from under his coat and held it out. Will received it as he lowered his own weapon. A soft sigh passed his lips. "You heard Hoyt. He quit. I'm the law now."

Beyond Deputy Spencer a second figure assumed substance. Jack recognized it as Tex Connelly. He made fast conversation to cover the Texan's approach, and, when he saw Will's eyes widen, his body draw up slightly, he stopped talking. Connelly's voice was a near whisper; it was saturnine-sounding.

"Now, Deputy, you hadn't ought to disarm a man at a time like this. It ain't sportin'." Tex looked over at Jack. "I can knock him over the head," he said.

Spencer broke in. "Wait a minute. Jack, did you

see that feller Hoyt was talkin' to out in the roadway a little while ago, the feller with the bowler hat?"

"I saw him. What of it?"

"He's the Yuma warden. He come up here after Hoyt went down to talk to him about you." The deputy's narrowed glance held steady. "He's in the hotel, waitin'."

"Waiting for what?"

"For you to walk out into the road against Josh Logan with a gun in your belt."

The sounds of dissension from within the office were growing louder. Jack had to raise his voice to be heard over them. "You're saying that's why you disarmed me . . . to keep him from . . . ?"

"Partly that. Partly because I don't want to see Hoyt do something wrong." Spencer relaxed. Behind him, Tex Connelly lowered his gun. He was straining to hear the argument in progress in Logan's office.

"I don't care who kills Logan," Spencer went on. "I could almost do it myself. I just don't think he's worth your future and the future of Sheriff Farmer. He's ruined a lot of men in his time. He'll ruin both of you two. You, if you're carrying a gun when you face him. Hoyt, if he even draws against him."

Tex shuffled his feet. "Jack, listen. Logan's comin' out."

The three of them faced toward the office. From beyond the door raised voices erupted in fierce contention. The door opened and a man stepped out. He was wearing a ragged windbreaker and had both arms high over his head. He called out in a reedy voice.

"Don't shoot! I surrender."

He walked out into the roadway and turned around slowly. "Sheriff . . . somebody . . . I surrender."

From the dripping darkness of a doorway Hoyt Farmer said: "Walk toward the jailhouse and keep your hands high."

A second railroader came then, followed by two more. One of them held a gun belt. As he stepped off the plank walk into the roadway, he dropped it in the dust. This time it was Calabasas who directed them toward the jail.

Beside Jack, the left-handed deputy raised his voice. It carried the full length of the roadway.

"Hold your fire! Everybody . . . don't shoot! Logan . . . you and the other railroaders come out with your hands high. Logan, you hear me?"

The reply was sharp. "I hear . . . and I'm not walking out of here to be shot down."

"You won't be . . . unless you force a fight. Come on out!"

Jack moved away from the wall for a better view of the office doorway. Tex Connelly was beside him, on the left. On his right stood Deputy Sheriff Will Spencer. The three of them, standing close together, completely barred the plank walk.

The utter stillness drew out. A short, thick silhouette emerged from the hotel doorway, hesitated briefly, looking north toward the three men blocking the plank walk, then ducked back out of sight. Jack had only a fleeting glimpse of a bowler hat.

In the gloom of Buck's barn a lounging figure was joined by another shadow. One wore two holsters, with one being empty. The other figure, older, bent and bowlegged, was hugging a long-barreled rifle.

Down by the sheriff's office a tall, cadaverous man was holding a gun on several other men whose arms were rigidly skyward. Directly in front of him was a gray-headed older man, also with an empty holster. He was staring from a bleak face at the open door of Joshua Logan's office up the road.

Jack saw every detail clearly. He even heard the boards creak when someone inched forward in Logan's office. Then he saw the man emerge, looking southward. It was Will Spencer's voice that turned the man to stone.

"Mister, drop that gun!"

The railroader started to turn, caught himself, and let the pistol fall from his hand.

"Walk out in the road an' down to the jailhouse."

The only sound that followed was that of heavy footfalls on hard-packed earth.

Then Joshua Logan and the solitary remaining

railroader came out. Both wore gun belts. They came through the doorway opening side-by-side, heads up and moving. Jack's voice stopped them less than fifty feet away. They turned to face him.

"Logan . . . send that man away."

The superintendent's face filled with dark blood; the strange, overpowering fury he was capable of showed in fire points that flamed from his eyes.

"He stays, Swift!"

"It's not his fight."

Logan's lips curled. "It's any law-abiding man's fight." The hot eyes flicked down, then up again. "Where's your gun, Swift? You made a fatal mistake coming after me without one."

"For the last time . . . send that man away!"

Joshua Logan made no move to obey or reply. He drew up very straight. His lips scarcely moved.

"Swift!"

Logan was dropping into a crouch, his right hand streaking downward, when two explosions, one a fraction of a second ahead of the other one, blew the night apart.

Logan went back a step, bumped the man beside him whose one shot went high over the heads of the three men facing him, then he braced himself against the office doorjamb, staring at the big man. The uninjured railroader was bringing his gun to bear when Jack's voice knifed into the echoing stillness.

"Don't!"

Two cocked guns, one in either fist, loomed black and ready. The railroader, who hadn't tugged back the hammer for his second shot, stared in fascination at death. He slowly lowered his weapon—then dropped it.

Joshua Logan slid down the front wall of his office and went over gently onto his side. He was dead.

The first man across the road was the Sundance Kid. The second was beanpole-like Calabasas Kid. They both held cocked guns. Sundance pushed the ashen-faced, uninjured railroader aside and flopped Joshua Logan over with his boot toe. Then he sighed and holstered his gun.

"Just a mite rusty," he said. "Just a mite."

A man with a bowler hat pushed through the gathering throng. He went up to Jack and halted, looking down for a gun belt. There was none. On either side of the big man stood Tex Connelly and the left-handed deputy sheriff. Both were ejecting spent casings and replacing them with loaded ones. The warden's face crinkled in bewilderment. "I'd have sworn it was you who shot him, Swift. I was watching from the hotel doorway."

Will Spencer looked down his nose reprovingly. "Now just how in hell could Swift have killed him when he isn't even wearing a gun?"

Tex Connelly pushed his weapon toward the man in the bowler hat. "Take a look, mister. Go ahead, smell it. It's been fired . . . one shot. Smell the deputy's gun, too. It's also been fired. You'll find two slugs in Logan. One from his gun . . . one from my gun." Tex dropped the gun into his holster. "You've got to be hit on the head to get an idea, mister?" He turned away, saw Hoyt Farmer talking to Sundance and Calabasas at the edge of the plank walk, and sauntered toward them.

The warden removed his hat, scratched his head, put his hat back on, took Jack by the arm, and steered him away from the growing crowd. When they were twenty feet off, he said: "All right, Swift, I'll admit I came up here to make plumb sure you didn't break the law. I'll swear on the witness stand under oath you didn't have a gun on you. Now then . . . just exactly how did you do that?"

Jack ordinarily would have smiled at the older man's perplexity. Right then, the vision of Joshua Logan's look of astonishment was still too vivid, after he had been hit.

"I didn't have a gun, Warden. I haven't packed one since I came to Herd . . . except for a couple of hours tonight . . . and the deputy took that one away from me."

"Never mind that. How . . . ?"

"The deputy is left-handed."

"I saw that."

"He and the other feller are about my size. They were standing close beside me. My fingers were within inches of both their holstered guns. When Logan went for his gun, I drew both of theirs and shot him."

The warden looked past Jack where the deputy was talking with Hoyt Farmer and Tex Connelly. He wagged his head and said: "God damn!"

Jack left him standing there, went around the crowd to the edge of the walk. There Sundance threw him a mirthless smile. Will Spencer studied his face in silence and Hoyt Farmer didn't look at him at all. Jack thought the sheriff looked older than his years. A hand brushed his sleeve lightly. He looked around. It was Buck. He jerked his head and moved away. Jack followed him. The old man screwed up his face.

"You'd better get down to Amy's, son. She's fit t' be tied for worryin' over you."

"I reckon," the big man said, and turned away from the crowd, heading south through the dark dust of the roadway.

It was over. All over.

About the Author

Lauran Paine who, under his own name and various pseudonyms has written over a thousand books, was born in Duluth, Minnesota. His family moved to California when he was at a young age and his apprenticeship as a Western writer came about through the years he spent in the livestock trade, rodeos, and even motion pictures where he served as an extra because of his expert horsemanship in several films starring movie cowboy Johnny Mack Brown. In the late 1930s, Paine trapped wild horses in northern Arizona and even, for a time, worked as a professional farrier. Paine came to know the Old West through the eyes of many who had been born in the previous century, and he learned that Western life had been very different from the way it was portrayed on the screen. "I knew men who had killed other men," he later recalled. "But they were the exceptions. Prior to and during the Depression, people were just too busy eking out an existence to indulge in Saturday-night brawls." He served in the U.S. Navy in the Second World War and began writing for Western pulp magazines following his discharge. It is interesting to note that all of his earliest novels (written under his own name and the pseudonym Mark Carrel) were published in the British market and he soon had as strong a

237

following in that country as in the United States. Paine's Western fiction is characterized by strong plots, authenticity, an apparently effortless ability to construct situation and character, and a preference for building his stories upon a solid foundation of historical fact. *Adobe Empire* (1956), one of his best novels, is a fictionalized account of the last twenty years in the life of trader William Bent and, in an off-trail way, has a melancholy, bittersweet texture that is not easily forgotten. In later novels like *The White Bird* (1997) and *Cache Cañon* (1998), he showed that the special magic and power of his stories and characters had only matured along with his basic themes of changing times, changing attitudes, learning from experience, respecting nature, and the yearning for a simpler, more moderate way of life.

Center Point Publishing

600 Brooks Road ● PO Box 1
Thorndike ME 04986-0001 USA

(207) 568-3717

US & Canada:
1 800 929-9108
www.centerpointlargeprint.com